Time Adjusters
& Other Stories

20 Year Anniversary Edition

Bill Ectric

billectric

Time Adjusters and Other Stories
20 Year Anniversary Edition

This is a work of fiction. The characters and events in this these
stories are fictional.

"The Euro Witches" was first published in *Pattern Recognition* No.1
(X-Force Productions, 2016, Summer)
HOME | patternrecognition (nocturnaliris8.wixsite.com

ISBN 9798218480219

Library of Congress Control Number: 2024915585

LCSH: American Science Fiction. Time travel.

BISAC:
FIC028080 FICTION /Science Fiction/ Time Travel

Published by *billectric*

To my parents, Bill and Paula, and
my brother Jeff. We lived in a
home of love and magic.

Contents

Introduction

Julie Carpenter

I once read a story, I don't remember where, in which two brothers were given the choice to become either gigantic or miniature. One became a giant and walked the world in no time flat. He'd made his world so small that it bored him. But the one who chose to be ant-sized? His garden became a galaxy of so many dazzling sights that he'd never again have the power to be dull or apathetic. It turned out that a world that had seemed so small to him before was a universe unto itself.

This is the feeling the reader has after encountering a Bill Ectric story. The world, which heretofore felt mundane, papered over with the monotony of necessity and everyday life, suddenly yields hidden portals, places where time and space fold in on themselves.

In a Bill Ectric story, you can walk through a hedge and end up 20 miles away or 20 years away, in an instant. But not every story makes you re-experience time and space. Bill's genius is that he understands there is no such thing as mundanity.

These stories are beautifully written gems that vary in genre, even containing some poetry. But each story has at its center the same playful depth. The author has caught onto some *game afoot* in the universe, some larger scheme that his characters (and by extension, his readers) can almost understand. There is meaning—whether you call it God, or infinity, or any other name—pulsing and teeming just beyond view.

Bill writes characters are real people who are open to experiences, who don't mind pulling at threads, even if they are overwhelmed by what they unravel. More than that, Bill, an existential Christian, finds a moral center that holds even as the universe threatens to unravel. The universe may be boundless, but it still contains love and decency.

Big and small, universal and personal come together in these stories to form concrete and recognizable events even as they suggest mysteries beyond, like an ordinary door set in a garden wall. When you leave these stories, you take away the feeling that there's mystery and vastitude in the commonplace. That there's a connection to the furthest reaches of time and space right around the corner or even closer. Every mind contains galaxies and eons.

You will walk away after reading these stories with the idea that if the universe isn't bigger than what we see, then it jolly well ought to be. Bill Ectric is stretching it at every corner.

Julie Carpenter 10 August 2024

Julie Carpenter is author of the linked short story collection, *Things Get Weird in Whistles*top. The book won the FAPA (Florida Authors and Publishers Association) 2020 silver medal for general fiction. Her prose has been published in Fiction on the Web and the New Guard Literary Anthology, Volumes VII and X. She is the administrator of Sacred Chickens Website and Blog page, a site that publishes book reviews, original stories, poems, and blog pieces. She has a Master of Arts in Professional Writing from the University of Memphis and currently works as a freelance content provider.

Foreword

Mikael Covey

Whatever our reaction to Bill Ectric's work, there is one thing we will all take away from the new *Time Adjusters* - the man can write. He can tell a story and make it spell binding, accessible, artful, and above all, worth our time. There are two rules to the written word. Catch the reader's fancy and be worth the time.

There is a publicity photo on his web site that shows the names of four writers pouring into Bill's head through a funnel. The writers are Edgar Allan Poe, Philip K. Dick, William S. Burroughs, and Kurt Vonnegut. I would add P. G. Wodehouse for his zany situational humor, and Lewis Carroll for his deceptively childlike forays into darkness. But mainly, I would (and did) tell Bill he should step out from underneath that funnel and let his own light shine. Every story in this book is a gem, uniquely different, surprising, and amazing.

The title story, "Time Adjusters," is cinematic; the settings, the characters, and the plot all lend themselves to the medium of film. My favorite is "The Little Robot," because it's from the heart, not the head. "The Little Robot" is Bill Ectric's turn to carry the Ray Bradbury torch.

If you're lucky enough to have read the previous Ectric collections, the original *Time Adjusters*, and *Space Savers*, then you have the pleasure of comparing the new versions with the old. There'll be debate and personal preference as to which you like better but in the final analysis you can't beat good writing.

Mikael Covey 15 March 2013

Mikael Covey is an American fiction writer and the founding editor of **Lit Up Magazine**. His published works include two novels, ***Out There*** and ***Princessa***, and numerous online short stories, poems, reviews, and opinion pieces.

Space Savers

Did you ever have a family member who seemed perfectly sane and reasonable in every way, except for when they claimed to see the ghost of their dead spouse? When I was a kid, it gave me the creeps when Grandma Cole said she saw her late husband Wayne.

Wayne, or as we called him, Grandpa Cole, died of heart failure in his workshop in the back yard of my grandparents' house. When he didn't come inside at bedtime, Grandma Cole went out and found him slumped over his workbench.

Two weeks after Grandpa's funeral, we were visiting Grandma Cole. My Mom and Dad, my five-year old brother Jeff, and I, age ten, were all sitting in Grandma's living room.

Out of nowhere, Grandma Cole said, "I saw him a few days ago."

"Saw who, Mama?" asked my father.

"Wayne."

"What do you mean?"

"I was in the den, last Tuesday night, watching the news. I got up off the sofa, turned off the TV, and was headed to bed. When I walked into the hallway, Wayne was standing there, in the bedroom doorway. He looked like he wanted to say something."

"Oh, Mama," said my father softly.

"I screamed!" declared Grandma. "I screamed and fainted, right there in the hallway."

My father said, "Maybe it was a dream."

"No," she said calmly. "No, I've dreamed about Wayne since he died, but this wasn't a dream. I saw him standing there when I was awake."

My brother and I looked at each other. I started to say something but my father caught my eye and shook his head. The subject passed, but Grandma Cole told that story more than once over the years, even after she moved into the Elm Shade Nursing Home, and her story never varied.

Once a month, a bus from the Elm Shade Nursing Home rolls up in front of the Publix grocery store, where I recently became Manager. A group of elderly men and women, including Grandma Cole, invade the grocery store, accompanied by a couple of caretakers. Some of the old folks leave their walkers at customer service and use shopping carts to steady themselves. One little granny wears slippers and a bathrobe wrapped over pajamas, but most of them dress more-or-less properly for this outing. A withered man wearing a pale green 1970s leisure suit has a gauze pad taped over the entire side of his head. After the man walks by and is out of earshot, two of my bag boys speculate as to whether or not the man's ear is missing.

Then one of the bag boys looks toward the entrance and says, "Here come the Borg Twins!"

People cringe in embarrassment at the phrase "Borg Twins," being a Star Trek reference to creatures that are part human and part machine. Nevertheless, the two old men smile and wave like celebrities at the bagboys. They don't mind the nickname, being old science fictions buffs themselves who play chess together and debate everything from the merits of Ray Bradbury versus Isaac Asimov to the theories of evolution versus creation. The "Borg Twins" are two old fat guys, Pops and Agee, who can't breathe normally because they have emphysema, so they carry portable oxygen tanks in the top section of their shopping carts. Plastic air tubes run from the oxygen tanks to their nostrils. Borgs. They stroll side by side, each pushing a shopping cart, basking in latter-day recognition by youthful nerds.

"How's it going, Pops?" asks a bagboy.

"It sucks!" says Pops, a real wise-ass.

Pops is bald on top, with wild tufts of white hair sticking out over his ears, bushy eyebrows, sloping nose and forehead, and a wide grin.

Loudly, Pops proclaims, "I'm thinkin' about hopping a freight train outta here!"

Agee smiles quietly. He is a black man, not quite as fat as Pops, who sports a beret, a goatee, and bifocals with heavy rectangular frames of dark burgundy.

Pops and Agee continue speaking to the bag boys as they plod along, pushing the shopping carts with oxygen tanks in them.

"What's the problem, Pops?" asks a bagboy.

"That damned loony bin they keep us in, that's what! How would you like to live with all those crazy motherfuckers?"

Agee says, "Watch your damn language, Pops."

"Oh, by all means!" says Pops sarcastically. "I wouldn't want to corrupt these unblemished lambs!"

As they shuffle past the bagboy, Agee looks at the teenager and chuckles, "Got to keep the loonies on the path."

"Hey, that's from Pink Floyd," says the bagboy. "You know Pink Floyd?"

"Sure!" says Agee.

"Yeah," adds Pops. "Wish you were here!"

Both men walk on toward the produce department, laughing.

When you were a child, did you ever think something should be true, and in spite of all logic, you almost believed it was true because it seemed right? For example, even though it took ninety minutes by car to get from my family's house to my grandparents' house, I thought maybe the houses were really side-by-side, separated by only a tall hedgerow. My basis for the idea was simple. A scary old woman named Mrs. Buttner lived at the end of our street and the tall, squarely trimmed row of shrubs in her yard looked just like the row of shrubs that backed my grandparents' property. I imagined that we drove for ninety minutes on some convoluted route, which eventually, subtly took us back to our own neighborhood, whereas if one were able to go into Mrs. Buttner's yard and sneak through the hedge, one would emerge in my grandparents' yard immediately on the other side! By way of confirming this theory, I set out to make it a reality to my younger brother, Jeff.

We arrived at my grandparents' house and after the prerequisite greetings, hugging, and shaking of hands, everyone went out back. The parents and grandparents sat on the back porch sipping drinks while my younger brother Jeff and I played in the yard. "Playing" consisted mainly of Jeff toddling around and me filling his head with bullshit.

"You see those shrubs?" I asked Jeff.

"Yeah."

"Well," I said. "If you crawl through those shrubs, you'll come out on the other side in Miss Buttner's yard. Remember the shrubs in her yard?"

"Yeah," he said.

"They're the same shrubs."

Young though he was, Jeff suspected trickery, but a couple of wasp nests prevented him from calling my bluff.

"Why does it take so long to get here?" he asked.

"Road and pavement regulations," I told him with a hint of scorn in my voice, as though he should have known it. "No streets can intersect past the city limits so we have to go around. When the Federal Government finishes building the Interstate Highway System, we can get here a lot quicker. Didn't you hear Dad say so?"

Here was the genius of my assertion. We always heard our parents and grandparents talking about how much time the Interstate would shave off the trip.

In fact, the advent of Interstate 81 reduced our travel time from ninety minutes to fifty minutes, nowhere near as instantaneous as the mythical shrub passage would have been, had it existed.

Years later, I learned that space could trick me in just the opposite way. Landscape design can create the facades necessary for Americans to feel like we still live in the wide-open spaces of our ancestors. I was surprised, for example, to learn how close the little league baseball field was to my house.

Bonnie and I had bought a small, cinderblock house in a nicely shaded, lower-middle-class neighborhood. It was perfect for us. For one thing, the price was right. The banks would not approve us for a house with two bathrooms or a pool. Also, we felt comfortable in this neighborhood. The people seemed less judgmental than, say, the residents of those gated communities that don't allow cars up on blocks or weirdly painted houses. Our neighbor across the street drove a van with "Lawn Care Larry" airbrushed on the side.

Driving to work every morning, I had to crisscross the neighborhood through several blocks of residential streets just to get to the main road, which had four traffic lights, followed by the Lakeshore Bridge. After crossing the short bridge, I could look to my left and see the Elm Shade Retirement Home, where my grandmother lived, followed by the Lakeshore Little League ball field. A block further, at a four-way intersection, I made a right turn into the Publix parking lot.

Soon after we moved in, the neighborhood had a 4th of July block party. By sunset, the whole street rocked with music, people talking, drinking beer, and shooting off illegal fireworks. Kids ran up and down the street waving sparklers. Bonnie and I stood in the middle of the road talking to Larry and his wife, Kyoko.

That's when I saw the unearthly glow in the distance, over the treetops.

"What the hell is that?" I asked in awe.

"Lights from the ball field," said Larry. "Lakeshore Little League."

"Oh, yeah," I said. "I drive past it on the way to work. I didn't think it was so close."

"The landscape can trick you," said Larry. "We used to play in those woods when I was a kid. Our tire swing is still there."

"Oh, I want to see it," said Bonnie.

"I'll get my flashlight and four more beers," said Larry.

Bonnie and I walked with Kyoko and Larry to the cul-de-sac at end of the street, where a small dirt path lead into what Larry called "the woods."

"These woods took up a few acres when I was a kid," said Larry as we walked. "A lot of it's been cut down."

The path ended in a small open space where an old tire hung by a rope from a high tree limb.

"Fifteen years ago," said Larry, "When I was ten or eleven years old, I climbed up that tree and out onto that limb, with the end of the rope tied to one of my belt loops. I lowered the rope down to a kid named Eddie Johnson. He tied the tire to it and hoisted it up by the other end of the rope, to the right height, and I wound it around the limb a few times and tied it as tight as I could. And further on, through that dense, thorny brush, which I don't recommend walking into, you'd see what's left of a fort we made from a couple of shipping crates."

"They must have been big crates," said Bonnie.

"Not really. See, that's the thing. When we were kids, they seemed big. I mean, to us it was this grand fort, you know? However, a few years later, we went back and I almost thought we were in the wrong spot. Just two dinky boxes, falling apart, covered with lichens.

Man, we used to see owls, foxes, all kinds of things out here, but not anymore."

That was a few years ago.

Recently, people have been seeing more snakes in their yards and in parking lots. It was on the local Six O'clock News. Construction companies are cutting down the small, wooded areas to build more housing developments, and this was driving snakes, turtles, and armadillos from their natural habitats.

The dirt path at the end of my street is no longer a dead end. It extends past brand-new houses, where the woods and rope swing used to be, and connects to the road beside the ball field. Now I can walk to work quicker than I could drive. It is almost a magical feeling, as if that impossible childhood thing had come true.

As if snakes, turtles, and armadillos weren't enough, there was an outbreak of "ghost sightings" in town, mainly concentrated on my side of town. A local radio station featured an interview with Dale Kaczmarek, the President of the Ghost Research Society. Did you ever hear of the strange, yet documented, story of the two men who died aboard the SS Watertown?

"The incident on the SS Watertown," said Mr. Kaczmarek, "Was recounted by the eminent and long-time director of the American Psychical Institute, Dr. Hereward Carrington, and detailed in the house magazine of the shipping company. A tanker ship, SS Watertown, was making its way through the Pacific Ocean in December 1924. Seaman James Courtney and Michael Meehan were assigned to clean out a cargo tank. While doing the task they were overcome by gas fumes and died before help could reach them. Following the tradition of the sea, their bodies were committed to the ocean on December 4th. The following day, just before dusk, the entire ship was in uproar when the heads of the two dead seamen were clearly seen on board ship and, later, in the sea. Thereafter the ghost faces were frequently seen, sometimes in the water."

This story gave me chills. It had a ring of truth to it, because of my own time in the Navy, in my early twenties. Our ship, the frigate USS Underwood, chanced upon a small yacht, half-sunk, floating aimlessly in the North Atlantic Ocean, near the Caribbean. When our rescue party boarded the yacht, they found no survivors, only five corpses, partially mummified and preserved by the salt water. The night before this happened, I had dreamed of mummies rising from the depths of the ocean, breaking vertically through surface of the water before falling sideways and floating away from each other in every direction.

The radio station asked Dale Kaczmarek to visit the Elm Shade Retirement home because of unexplained shadowy figures reported by patients and staff; however, the retirement home administration steadfastly refused to cooperate with any investigation, stating that it might stress out the residents.

Did you ever lay in bed after having sex with your wife and talk about future plans? One exultant night, I rolled onto my back and dropped the used condom on my side of the bed, between the bed and the wall.

"Tell me you didn't just drop that on the floor," said Bonnie, disgusted.

"I'll pick it up later," I said, and then tried to make it sound romantic with, "Right now I just want to lay here, with you."

"That's an excuse for laziness, and you are nasty."

"You know what we need?" I asked.

"What? A trash can on your side of the bed?"

"No. This house needs more than one bathroom. We need a bathroom connecting right here," I said, tapping the wall beside me on my right. "I could get out of bed and walk right into the bathroom."

"Yeah," said Bonnie. "Well, how much would something like that cost?"

"Not much if I did it myself," I said. "I bet Larry would help me. Knock out part of this wall for a door…there's plenty of room in the backyard for an extension."

"Oh, look at that," she said.

"What?"

The TV was on at low volume. Bonnie reached for the remote and turned up the sound so we could find out why the Elm Shade Nursing Home was on the Eleven O'clock News.

Taped earlier that day, a woman wearing sunglasses and a scarf spoke with a heavy Brooklyn accent to a reporter. We could see the Elm Shade Nursing Home in the background.

The woman said, "It was never a problem in the past! I could come here and visit my mother any time I felt like it! Now, just because they are closing…"

"What?" I said. "Elm Shade is closing?"

"Shhhh!" said Bonnie.

The Brooklyn lady continued, "My job switches me from day shift to evening shift and then back again. I need flexibility when it comes to visiting my mother here at the Home."

The news reporter concluded the segment, speaking to the camera, "A spokesman for the Elm Shade Nursing Home told us that the more restrictive visitation schedules are a result of increased concerns for the safety of the Home's residents. Elm Shade has confirmed that they will soon close their doors permanently, but they assure the public that they will work with each and every family in relocating their loved ones to other suitable retirement homes."

"That must be what the letter is about," I said.

"What letter?"

"From Elm Shade."

"You got a letter from the nursing home?" chided Bonnie. "And didn't open it?"

"I was going to open it," I said. "They send a newsletter every month, usually asking for volunteers or donations."

"Well, tomorrow I guess you'll have to read it and find out what day and time you can visit your grandmother."

"That's bullshit," I said. "I agree with the woman on TV. I'll visit my grandmother whenever I feel like it."

"Which is…hmmm…almost never?" said Bonnie

"I know, I know. I'll stop by and see her tomorrow, after work," I said. "What's tomorrow, Friday?"

"Yeah, Larry and Kyoko are coming over tomorrow evening. We're cooking out on the grill."

"Perfect," I said. "That'll be my excuse not to stay too long."

"You're terrible," joked Bonnie.

The next day, a strange atmosphere of curiosity mingled with apprehension filled the lobby of the Elm Shade Nursing Home. People milled around in the lobby, waiting to see someone, or filling out paperwork, or complaining quietly about the new visiting restrictions.

At the counter, a middle-aged woman with heavy make-up and a bejeweled chain hanging from her eyeglasses asked, "How may I help you, sir?"

"I'm here to sign papers to transfer my grandmother, Katherine Cole, to Baptist Retirement Village."

"Ah, yes, transfer authorization. Do you have the acceptance form from Baptist?"

"They said they would fax it to you."

"Oh?" she said, in that tone of concern and puzzlement so often heard in medical facilities when the simple processing of paperwork is involved.

"Yes," I said. "Maybe you have it?"

"I'll have to check. I'm sorry. It will only take a moment."

"Would it be okay if I went, just for a minute, to say hi to my grandmother?"

"Well, we have to check the schedule," the woman said, tapping on her keyboard. "Let me see, Cole is the last name? Oh, this darn computer…ah, there it goes… C, O, L, E… "

"I know where her room is."

"I'm sure you do," said the woman. "It's a safety concern, sir, and they're very strict about it. Ohhh, dear, it shows your visiting hour is Sunday, in the courtyard…"

"I just want to go to her room. I could have already been there and back!"

"I know it sounds picky, but your visitation site is the courtyard, and the garden paths in the courtyard are regulated for safety. If we exceed the capacity, we get fined."

"For God's sake, it's not a night club!" I said a bit louder than I intended.

"There's a greater risk of injury, sir," insisted the woman.

A man behind me said, "You're fightin' a losing battle, sport."

I turned to see a burley but good-natured police officer, in uniform.

"What?" I asked.

"I said you might as well not argue the point. This lady is just doing her job, it's not her fault."

"What, they have Police now to keep people from seeing their grandparents?"

"I'm here to see MY mother," said the cop. "And don't get smart with me."

The woman behind the counter was watching us both, and finally said quietly, "It's the ones who flaunt the rules that are usually the quickest to sue when someone gets hurt."

The cop looked at me and shrugged.

"Fine," I said. "Where's the form I came here to sign?"

"Well, let's see," said the woman. "Do you have the acceptance form from Baptist, or, did I already ask you that?"

"They said they FAXED it to you."

"Oh? I'll have to find out if we can accept a faxed copy. It really should be the original or a certified copy. Did they say which number they faxed it to?"

"How about if I sign your form now and bring you the other form Sunday when I visit my grandmother?"

"Our business office is not open on Sundays. You would need to bring it on Monday."

"Fine."

"But that won't be possible, either," she said. "We'll be completely closed down by then, and everyone will have been transferred to their new residences."

I signed something and went home to drink a beer and prepare for the cookout.

The doorbell rang.

"Hey, it's Lawn Care Larry and his wife, Lawn Care Kyoko!" I said when I opened the front door. "Come in, folks."

It rained, so we all sat in the living room, eating hamburgers and potato salad from paper plates. I told Larry I wanted to expand my house.

"Best thing to do," he said, "Is put up a big mirror. Mirrors make the place look twice as big."

"Great," I said. "Then I can just piss on the mirror and watch it splash back on me."

"What?" His disgusted face made me laugh. "What the fuck is wrong with you?"

Bonnie said, "He wants to add a bathroom, Larry."

"Well, why didn't you say so? Jeez!"

Bonnie said, "But you know, a mirror *would* look good on that wall."

Kyoko said, "In Japanese, my names means "mirror."

"Really?" said Bonnie.

"It's true," said Larry. "I looked it up."

"Cool," I said. "Hey, I hear they really have a space problem in Japan."

"Space problem?" asked Larry.

"Oh, you mean limited space," said Kyoko. "That's true. The population is dense."

"Yeah," said Larry. "We took a course on that when I was stationed over there. About the bubble."

"Bubble?" I asked.

"The bubble of personal space," said Kyoko.

"Yeah," Larry continued. "Americans have what we call bubble of personal space around us. The Japanese don't have room for that, so they make their own personal space inside their head."

"Is that true, Kyoko?" asked Bonnie.

"Well, sort of, yeah," Kyoko said. "The Japanese are much more respectful of each other in public. We speak softly. We use earphones to listen to music. Things like that."

"I feel like getting away from people some days," I said.

"The way my father taught me," said Kyoko, "Is like this: If you go to a park that has trees, flower gardens, fountains and statues, when you are walking through the park, you can only be in one place at any given time. What difference does it make if many people are walking in the same park, each following a different path, as long as they do not bump into each other?"

"But I don't like crowds," I said.

"There would be no crowd in your mind," said Kyoto. "Everyone minds their own business."

"Stupid Elm Shade must have more people than it does paths," I remarked.

"What do you mean?" asked Larry.

"On the way home from work, I went there to sign papers to have Grandma transferred to the Baptist Retirement Village."

"Oh, that's right," said Kyoko. "We saw on the news that Elm Shade is closing."

"Yeah," I said. "Well, they wouldn't let me visit her!"

"They stopped you from seeing your grandmother?" said Larry. "I would have told them to kiss my ass. I'm going to see my Grandma, damn it."

"I did! I almost got arrested!" I exaggerated.

"You've got to be kidding," said Larry.

Bonnie said, "It's basically about risk management. Apparently, they have some garden paths in the courtyard and if too many people walk these paths at the same time..."

"Some old fogey will get knocked down and break a hip?" I completed her sentence.

Larry laughed, "Got to keep the loonies on the path!"

Kyoko said, "Larry! That's not very nice."

"It's Pink Floyd!" said Larry defensively. "From *Dark Side of the Moon*."

"Pops quoted the same thing!" I said.

"Who?"

"An old man from the Home!"

"Oh, really?" asked Larry. "Some old geezer was quoting Pink Floyd?"

"Yeah, old Pops is a trip!" I said.

Bonnie said, "Maybe that's what he was talking about. The paths in the courtyard."

"Well, no wonder they're closing," said Larry.

Did you ever act on a premonition?

One night I had to work late at the grocery store, supervising the stock crew while the regular night guy was out sick. It was almost midnight when we finished.

Driving home, I probably would not have paid any attention to the Elm Shade Retirement Home had they not recently pissed me off. I slowed down and glowered at the building as I drove past it.

Every window in the wide, flat brick building was dark, except for the glass doors to the main entrance. In the light of the lobby, a security guard sat behind the reception desk reading a newspaper. A single streetlight cast shadows of shrubbery onto the side of the building.

Suddenly, one of the shadows moved.

I stopped in the road, squinting at the side of the building. Someone was crouching down between the wall and the shrubs, creeping toward the back of the retirement home. I did not know if they saw me watching, so I drove a little further until I was out of their line of sight and parked on the side of the road. I sprinted quietly to the left side of the building and crept along the left wall, toward the back of the building, while the other figure presumably moved along the right wall in similar fashion.

I eased my head around the rear corner of the building ever so slowly. There was the mystery prowler, a tall man dressed in all black, and wearing a black wool stocking cap. He walked briskly from the far corner of the building, along the rear wall, toward me. I thought for a moment he had seen me, but he stopped midway along the wall and disappeared into an entrance.

I approached the entrance and saw that it was an archway covered with vines. The archway led to the courtyard paths. These paths were technically outdoors, but trellised vines everywhere gave the feeling of enclosure. Soft moonlight filtered through the vine canopy, but even so, I could barely see where I was going. I hid behind a marble statue and watched the tall man as he scanned the ground with his flashlight.

The flashlight beam paused on a flat rock beside the path. The person knelt down on one knee and laid his flashlight on the ground with the beam still shining on the rock. With one hand, he lifted the rock to a 45 degree angle, reached underneath with the other hand removed a small package from a hole in the ground. He let the rock drop back over the hole, stood up with his flashlight and the package, and walked out through the archway as briskly as he had walked in. I had to rotate my position behind the marble statue to stay hidden as he walked by, but I got a glimpse of long, bushy sideburns extending down past the wool cap.

What was that all about? I wondered.

A peculiar sensation crept over me - the feeling that I was not alone.

I turned and looked down the dimly lit path. Something moved in the distance.

For a moment, I doubted my own eyes.

The pale form of an elderly, obese man in a hospital gown, spectral in the moonlight, shuffled toward me.

When the old man came closer, I could see his mouth stretched open in a repulsive silent scream. The horror in his eyes made my skin crawl.

Less than ten feet away, he stretched his arms toward me, knotted knuckles clutching at the air between us. I swear I could see right through him. I backed away to avoid his grasping hands.

I had been hiding behind what I later learned was a statue of Saint Francis of Assisi. In the dark, I did not see the little animal statues flocking around the saint's marble feet. Backing up, I tripped over a stone rabbit and hit the ground painfully, knocking the breath out of me.

Rolling onto my side, I looked up, expecting to see the old man on top of me. He was gone.

"Where have you been?" Bonnie was still awake when I finally got home, way after midnight.

"The retirement home," I said wearily.

"The home? Because of the missing guy?"

"Yeah. I mean no. What did you just say?"

"The missing guy," said Bonnie. "One of the residents, a Mr. Finnegan, wandered off and nobody knows where he is."

"No, I didn't know about that. Did he have Alzheimer's or something?"

"I don't know, but his family is not very happy with Elm Shade."

"You won't believe what happened to me. It was crazy."

The next day, I put the assistant manager in charge of the grocery store and went to the Baptist Retirement Village.

"I'm here to see my grandmother, Mrs. Katherine Cole," I told the receptionist. "She was transferred here from Elm Shade."

"Of course," said the receptionist. "Mrs. Cole is in room 211. The elevator is down that hall to your right. I believe a detective is speaking to her now."

"A detective?"

"Yes. About the gentleman who went missing from Elm Shade."

I took the elevator to the second floor, wondering what in the world my grandmother would know about Finny Finnegan. The heavy wooden door to room 211 was halfway closed. Hearing a man's voice, I pushed the door open quietly. I saw my grandmother, propped up comfortably by pillows in her bed. The detective sat politely in a chair between the bed and window, legs crossed in that formal way of lanky gentlemen in suits, one knee over the other, and a notepad resting on the top knee.

I walked into the room.

"Well, look who it is!" said Grandma. "Detective Poole, this is my son, Bill."

Holding the notepad and pen in his left hand, Detective Poole stood up and reached across the bed to shake my hand. He was tall and vigorous, middle-aged with a receding hairline, long sideburns, and a youthful glint in his eye that seemed to wink when he smiled.

"Pleased to meet you," he said, before sitting down again. "We're speaking to all the former occupants of Elm Shade about Mr. Finnegan, the missing resident."

Unexpectedly, Grandma said, "My husband Wayne told me Finny Finnegan was lost."

"Grandma," I interrupted.

"Does your husband live here at Baptist?" asked Poole.

Grandma looked at me and said, "My grandson will not like what I'm about to say."

Detective Poole looked at me, then back at her.

I spoke to her softly, the way I remembered my father speaking to her, "Grandpa passed away."

"I know that, baby," she said. "My husband Wayne has passed from this world to the next." Then she looked at the detective and added, "But he visits me sometimes."

Detective Poole surprised me with his answer. He said, "We sometimes rely on psychics to solve puzzling cases, Mrs. Cole. Perhaps this is similar."

"The first time Wayne appeared to me," she said, "was shortly after he died. I was in the den watching TV on a Tuesday evening. I got up off the sofa, turned off the TV, and was going to bed. When I walked into the hallway, Wayne was standing there, in the bedroom doorway. He looked like he wanted to say something. I screamed!"

Detective Poole said, "Maybe it was a dream."

"No," said Grandma Cole calmly. "No, I've dreamed about Wayne since he died, but this wasn't a dream. I saw him standing there when I was awake. The first time I saw him, I was afraid. After that, it was okay. When I moved into Elm Shade, I was so sad because I thought I was leaving Wayne behind in the house. But there was no need to worry! He appeared to me at Elm Shade, the very first night I was there. And two nights ago, I saw him here at Baptist. He is free, not like that poor Mr. Finny."

"What do you mean?" asked Poole.

"Wayne said Mr. Finny is trapped at Elm Shade and can't leave."

"We've search Elm Shade thoroughly," said Detective Poole patiently. "Mr. Finnegan is not there, Mrs. Cole."

"He is in purgatory!" said Grandma Cole gravely. "Poor Mr. Finny is suffering in purgatory!"

The next day I was at the grocery store, yawning from lack of sleep, when Pops and Agee shuffled in, pushing their shopping carts with the oxygen tanks onboard.

I followed them down the medicine aisle, where they stopped at a shelf full of eye medication.

"You need the Visine," Pops said to Agee. "Got that red-eye from smoking dope."

"If anyone uses drugs, it's you, Pops," said Agee.

"Don't bullshit me," said Pops. "You listen to jazz and smoke grass!"

"Yeah, right," Agee shot back.

I walked up and said, "So, what's new, Borgsters?"

Agee smiled and nodded a hello, friendly eyes framed by thick burgundy eyeglasses.

Pops said, "Hey, young fellow! Agee here needs some generic Visine!"

"Shut up, Pops," said Agee with a smile.

I said, "What's this I hear about someone missing from Elm Shade?"

"Finny Finnegan," said Pops. "Finny's been missing for a couple of days."

"It's a cover-up," said Agee matter-of-factly.

"A cover-up?" I said.

Agee said, "Pops here thinks he saw Finny's ghost one night."

"He's still at the home," said Pops with a devious grin. "He never left. And he's no ghost!"

Agee said firmly, "Pops, what you described to me is a ghost."

Pops gave a wide-mouthed mocking laugh. "I'm a man of science!" he said.

"Oh," I said. "Are you saying a man of science can't believe in ghosts?"

"There are believers on both ends of the spectrum," said Pops. "Agee here is a retired pastor. He literally believes the Old Testament story in First Samuel, about a witch who talks to ghosts."

"That's right," said Agee matter-of-factly. "First Samuel, Chapter 28. King Saul consulted with a witch to summon up the ghost of Samuel."

I felt a tingle up my spine. I looked at Agee for a moment, and then turned to Pops.

"What do you believe, Pops?" I asked.

His bushy eyebrows arched upwards. "I believe that we are made of atoms, and atoms are made of protons, neutrons, and electrons, and…"

"Just say string theory," interrupted Agee, who looked at me and explained, "Otherwise he will go on all day."

"Maybe this young man doesn't know about string theory," said Pops indignantly.

They both looked at me.

"No," I said. "I don't."

Pops said, "You know everything has three dimensions, right?"

"Yeah," I said. "Height, width, and depth. Some people say the fourth dimension is time."

"That's an older theory," said Pops. "Scientists now believe there may be eleven dimensions. Time is still a part of it, though."

I said, "I never really understood how time could be a dimension."

"Well," said Pops, reaching for a box of Visine wrapped in cellophane. "Look at this box. When I lift it up off the shelf, imagine that it leaves a trail."

"A trail?" I asked.

"Yeah," said Pops. "You know, a box-shaped trail from where the Visine sat on the shelf, extending up to where I'm holding it now, twelve inches above the shelf. You do have an imagination, don'tcha? You can't really see the trail. You can only see the box in one place at a time."

He put the box back on the shelf, still holding it with his thumb and forefinger, and said, "You see it here," then lifting the box six inches, "and now you see it here. You saw it down there a couple of seconds ago. To see it in both places at once, you'd have to step out of time."

"Okay," I said. "So time is the fourth dimension?"

"Well, it would be, if there were only four dimensions," said Pops. "But if you can imagine a vertical trail when I lift the box straight up, you have to consider that the Earth is turning, so there is also a trail streaming sideways off the box as the Earth turns."

"So that is another dimension?" I asked.

"I think so," said Pops. "But that's not all. The Earth is not only spinning around, it is also traveling around the sun. That's *another* trail. And if you believe the theory that the universe is expanding, that's still another trail!"

Agee smiled knowingly. I realized that Agee understood Pops just fine; they just enjoyed picking on each other. He said, "Pops, tell him why we can only see three dimensions."

"Ahhhh," said Pops. "That's where string theory comes in. The study of quantum physics suggests that all these dimensions fold back on themselves. They're invisible to us!"

"That sounds crazy," I said.

"He didn't make this stuff up," said Agee. "There are mathematical formulas that back it up. There is an invisible world. Of course, I knew that from reading my Bible. Pops here had to get it from the Discovery Channel."

"Discovery Channel, my ass," said Pops. "I worked on the particle accelerator in Switzerland. If anything, the discovery channel learned it from me!"

I looked at Agee to see his reaction.

With a knowing smile, Agee said, "It all checks out with God's creation."

"What do you mean?" I asked.

"God made texture in everything," said Agee. "Did you know that if the inner lining of your intestines were smooth, they would only have about six square feet of surface area? But the fact is, the texture of those inner walls is such that if you could spread it out, it would be 4,000 square feet. It stands to reason that our entire universe is the same way – folding back on itself."

"And poor old Finny is lost in the folds!" said Pops.

"I think I saw him, too," I said. "But then again, it sounds impossible. Are you sure you guys aren't full of shit?"

"Well," said Pops, "If we are, then **Global Interlinear** sure has invested a lot of money in shit!"

"Global Interlinear," I said. "I think I've seen that name somewhere."

"I can tell you where you *didn't* hear it!" declared Pops. "On the radio!"

"Why would I hear it on the radio?"

"I said you wouldn't hear it, and you didn't."

I looked at Agee for a clue.

"Pops thinks Global Interlinear has been around since 1924. Something about that ship where the two sailors died."

"The SS Watertown," said Pops, lowering his voice. "Did you hear what that ghost hunter said on the newspaper?"

"Yeah," I said. "About the two guys who died on board the ship, and crewmembers reported seeing their faces everywhere."

"That tanker was chartered by the same corporation that later became Global Interlinear."

I looked at Agee, who simply shrugged and said, "Come on Pops, it's time for brunch."

So the Borg Twins left me to ponder where I had heard of Global Interlinear if certainly not on the radio.

Then it hit me.

In the grocery store, every available surface carries an ad. They even put ads on the floor between each aisle, glued down and laminated by some protective polymer to withstand thousands of shoes treading and shopping carts rolling. Those little plastic coupon dispensers stick out sideways from the shelves. As though the ad people discovered a new dimension to exploit. Not only are the shelves tall, wide, and deep – now they have ads that extend out into space where before there was nothing but air. In tiny letters, on all the coupon dispensers in my store, it says, **Global Interlinear Corporation®**. I did some research on the company.

Did you ever notice how big companies sometimes diversify into areas with which they formerly had no connection? For example, Lockheed Martin Corporation builds military aircraft, but recently, their information technology department has gone into the Child Support Enforcement business. They are bidding for contracts with several states that want to turn their Child Support departments over to private businesses.

It's a similar thing with Global Interlinear. They started out building particle accelerators so scientists could split atoms and try to observe quarks and other tiny bits of matter. Next, they branched into advertising. Then they purchased a whole chain of retirement homes. Their public relations literature spoke of innovative ways to solve problems of overcrowding.

I thought it was more than a coincidence that Detective Poole had long sideburns like the man I had seen sneaking around in the courtyard behind Elm Shade. I went to see the detective at the Police station. He invited me into his office.

"Have a seat," said Poole. "How can I help you?"

Have you ever wanted to say something significantly suggestive, to show that you were hip to a secret? I have, and I didn't want to miss my chance.

"During your search for the missing man," I said smugly, "I assume you left no stone unturned in the courtyard."

Poole did an almost imperceptible double take and looked quizzically at my face. Then he relaxed and leaned back in his chair.

"Ahhhh," said Detective Poole. "It was you. I thought I heard someone following me."

"I didn't do anything wrong," I said, my smugness turning quickly into fear of authority. "I was worried about my grandmother."

"I believe you," said Poole. "I caught the guy I was looking for."

"What was under the rock?" I asked.

"Pain medication," said Poole. "One of the orderlies was stealing boxes of drugs and stashing them under rocks in the courtyard. Later, he would come back and get them."

I felt like I was in on some secret Police matter.

"We've already arrested the guy," added the detective. "It's in the newspapers."

"I guess I've been too busy to read the papers," I said. "So, by any chance, was it an old man?"

"No, a young guy. An orderly. He tried to get a plea bargain by turning evidence on the retirement home. He told us he only stole medication from residents who were deceased."

"Deceased?"

"He said Elm Shade was covering up deaths, and not allowing people to visit their relatives because the relatives were dead. But his story didn't check out."

"What about Finny Finnegan?" I asked. "He's missing."

"Yes, and his family is suing Elm Shade's ass off. That's the main reason they're going out of business."

"Global Interlinear is going out of business?"

"No, no, they've got billions of dollars. They're just cutting their losses, getting out of retirement home business."

"Well, listen," I said. "I saw an old man in the courtyard that same night I saw you there!"

"That's hardly possible," said Detective Poole. "The place had been thoroughly searched by then."

"No wonder Elm Shade had strict visitation times," I told the detective. "They only had half the residents available at any given time. Maybe the others were there, but they were in the folds of space, where the dimensions fold back on themselves!"

"Where did you come up with that far-fetched notion?" asked Poole. "Your grandmother?"

I continued, "When Elm Shade came under scrutiny, they had to bring everyone back. You shut them down before they had time to bring back Finny Finnegan."

"A fantastic scenario," said Detective Poole sarcastically.

"You said yourself that sometimes you rely on psychics," I said. "How is this any more fantastic?"

"I didn't want to hurt your grandmother's feelings," said Poole. "But I don't really take that stuff seriously."

"You were pulling my grandmother's leg?"

"Yeah."

"What if that crazy stuff is true?" I asked.

"You want to believe it's true, don't you?" said Poole.

"I've always felt that there was something more," I said. "Something hidden from our sight. When I was a kid, I thought there was a space-warp between my parents' house and my grandparents' house."

"Oh, man," said Poole. "I thought the same thing!"

"It was in the shrub hedge," I said.

"Mine was the ocean. My mother and I lived near the ocean. So did my grandparents. When we visited my grandparents, we went by plane, but I always thought that if we had a boat we could get there quicker. You see, when I looked out at the ocean, I saw these trawlers on the horizon."

Detective Poole closed one eye and pointed his fingers at an imaginary little trawler in a distant sunset.

He continued, "Way out there, the trawlers always looked the same, whether I saw from my mother's house or my grandparents' house. I thought they were the same ships. I thought if we could just take a boat out there, past those fishing ships, my grandparents' house would come into view, just over the curve of the Earth."

"But they weren't the same ships?" I asked.

"No," he laughed. "They couldn't be. It wasn't even the same ocean. I grew up in Monterey, California. My grandparents were retired in Florida. I figured it out when I got older."

"Maybe children sense things that adults don't," I said.

"Maybe children are naïve and ignorant," laughed Poole.

That evening, I asked Lawn Care Larry to go with me to Elm Shade.

"It's not that I really believe all that shit about space folding back on itself," I said. "But something is going on. When I told the detective I saw that old geezer, he didn't even hesitate in saying I was wrong. As much as the police want to find Finny Finnegan, and here I am telling him I saw somebody in the courtyard, wouldn't you think he'd give me the benefit of the doubt and rush back over there?"

"Damn straight," said Larry. "Unless…maybe he didn't want you to know what they know! Do you think the old guy is still there?"

"Maybe," I said. "Maybe not. Either way, I can't get my mind off the place. I want to go back and check it out."

"Buy us a twelve pack of Budweiser and I'll do it," he said.

Bonnie and Kyoko insisted on going with us. We decided not to drive. We took the shortcut, walking down the neighborhood road, across the deserted baseball field, through the Publix parking lot. Larry and I carried the plastic beer cooler between us, by the handles on each end.

We stopped at a row of square-cut shrub hedges backed by a privacy fence.

"We're behind the Elm Shade retirement home," I said. "On the other side of this wall is the entrance to the courtyard."

We put our empty beer cans in the cooler with the rest of the full cans. Squeezing between two shrubs, we stood on the beer cooler to facilitate climbing over the wall.

"Leave the cooler," said Larry, when we all stood on inside the courtyard. "The shrubs will hide it."

Larry, shining one of those big Maglite flashlights like the ones the police carry, walked through the arched entrance first. Kyoko followed him, carrying one of those square flashlights with the handle on top.

Bonnie and I heard Kyoko say, "Larry! Where did you go?"

We looked at each other and walked through the entrance. As I said before, the wooden framework covered with vines formed a canopy that gave the area a semi-enclosed feeling. My keychain penlight beam darted all around against shrubs, benches, and statues as I searched for any sign of Kyoko and Larry, but I saw no one.

"Where are they?" I asked, but when I flashed my penlight in Bonnie's direction, she was gone, too. Stranger still, I couldn't see the entrance we had only seconds ago passed through. There was no longer a way out.

"Bonnie!" I called out.

No answer.

Have you ever stood between two full-length mirrors and seen that seemingly endless repetition of "rooms" generated by reflections of reflections of reflections? This is what I saw now, but with a terrifying difference. Old men and women, in shroud-like gowns, lumbered through the infinite mirror hall in both directions, like souls lost in purgatory.

In the distance, an old woman walked slowly in my direction, leaning on a handrail attached to the wall. Someone had tied her wrist loosely to the handrail with a strip of white cloth. I had seen this done before to keep senile patients from wandering when the orderlies were busy. She stopped and tugged at the cloth when one of the wall brackets blocked her advance. After a moment of facing the wall, the old woman turned around, the bound arm crossed in front of her, and padded slowly in the other direction, only to repeat these actions at the next bracket down.

A squinting, skeletal man, arms extended like a sleepwalker, groped at the air as if clearing cobwebs.

Someone sat in a wheelchair, wrapped from head to toe in a thick blanket, only their knobby hands visible as they struggled to roll the wheels forward, but only succeeded in rotating the chair slowly, 360 degrees one way and then back the other way, a corner of the thick blanket wedged under one wheel.

Someone walked up behind me and touched my shoulder. Startled, I turned around and saw a boney hand pull away quickly. My gaze followed an appallingly withered arm, afflicted with pustules, to the face of the old man I had the last time I was here. He was still in a hospital gown, but now, instead of obese, he looked emaciated, and loose skin hung from his arms and the jowls of his mummy-like face, filling me with a mixture of fear, pity, and revulsion.

I took a couple of steps backward and turned away from the old man. When I turned, my right arm disappeared up to the elbow! It felt like I had plunged my arm into a vertical pool of water, and in fact, I saw ripples on the invisible mirror pane, emanating from where my arm vanished. About ten feet away I saw my forearm, disembodied, floating, extended toward me from another vertical mirror surface. I extended my right arm further, until it disappeared up to the shoulder, and watched the disembodied forearm lengthen into an entire limb. Involuntarily, my shoulder and the side of my head crossed over into the mirror pane and I realized that some force was tugging at me, drawing me in. I tried to pull back, but the harder I pulled, the stronger it tugged at me, like an invisible, vertical pool of quicksand. I fought against an overwhelming urge to look at my body emerging from the opposite plane, sensing that once I saw my face over there, there would be no turning back.

But the urge was too strong. I looked. Expecting to see my own face, I saw only a one-armed, headless body in an unnatural half-crouch. The only thing to do now was to finish crossing over by walking all the way into the first mirror so my body could emerge whole from the mirror across the room.

The form of a running man suddenly entered my peripheral vision. The tall form tackled my body violently, virtually ripping me free from the energy sheet, and we both fell to the ground.

"Sorry I brought you down so hard," said Detective Poole. "It's like pulling a man off a live wire without getting yourself electrocuted. If you had crossed over, we might not have got you back."

Crazy lights danced all around us. It was Bonnie, Kyoko, and Larry, suddenly visible, waving their flashlights about. We were all standing within a few feet of one another.

"Where were you?" asked Larry.

"Where were you?" asked Kyoko.

The mirror panes and old people were gone. Everything looked normal again. Even the exit had reappeared.

Standing, Poole extended a hand to help me up.

"Why did the old people disappear?" I asked.

"Because," said the detective, "I shut down the Global Interlinear grid as soon as I got here, but it takes a couple of minutes to power down. It still had enough power to pull you in, obviously, even as it faded."

"What the *hell!*" demanded Larry.

"None of you are supposed to be in here," said Detective Poole with possibly a bit of anger in his voice. "Come on, let's go. Out, the way you came in."

Pool followed us back over the fence, where Larry immediately started handing out beer from the cooler to everyone. He offered a beer to the detective, who waved it off.

"Can't the Police shut that thing down for good?" I asked.

"We thought we *did*," said Poole. "But we had to boot it up again when we realized some people were missing."

"Some people?" I asked.

"Yeah," said the detective. "I guess there's no reason not to tell you now. We haven't released this to the public. Finnegan was the only one whose family blew the whistle on Elm Shade, but according to records we found, there are others missing."

"Others what?" asked Larry, wiping beer from his chin.

"Missing."

"How could that be?" I asked. "What about their families?"

"The best we can tell," said Poole, "The other missing residents have no close family members living in the city. Or maybe anywhere. We're still looking."

The next day, the Police found the body of Finny Finnegan, still in his hospital gown. The coroner's report said that Finnegan had been dead, from starvation, for almost a week.

I don't know which mystery is harder to explain: That Finnegan could appear to me when he was already dead, or how living people could disappear into the folds of another dimension.

State Troopers guard the supposedly empty Elm Shade Retirement Home around the clock.

The House and the Baboon

Part 1

A haunted house would make a good article, I thought. I called in sick on Tuesday, drank some coffee, and sat down to write. My wife went to work. Now it was 10:30 AM, which is like a magic hour when you call in sick because it's not too late, plenty of possibility left in the day, and usually some good TV shows come on about this time. Old reruns, sensational talk shows, and Judge's Court. But I'm not watching the judge today. I have a story to write about the haunted house across the street.

It is not a traditional haunted house; it's a Florida haunted house, meaning there is a window on the second floor shaped like a porthole that seems to scream shrilly at you when you walk past it at night. Then there's the old dead coconut tree and the rusted anchor someone put in the yard years ago for decoration. The scarred up door that's been broken into and patched up twice. Nobody has lived there for seven years, which is strange. There has never been a For Sale sign in the front yard. People say it's haunted because of inexplicable incidents, like when some kids snuck in for kicks and came out all freaked about a "hairy legged" apparition they saw. I don't know what the hell they saw.

To write, I took a pill to wake me up along with the coffee.

I was also waiting on the Sears Plumber to fix my clogged sewer pipe. I was getting very pissed off because the plumber was late. They are always late.

I got out there in the yard and dug up part of the pipe but the glaring, hot sun sent me scurrying for air-conditioned cover. The only thing I hate about Florida is the sun.

Now I'm waiting for the plumber and I'm on edge.

I needed something to take the edge off. My wife's gay cousin Mark was living next door with my biker neighbors, Big'n and Fran. Mark had been kicked out of his last house over a misunderstanding involving dope. He had pawned his roommate's TV while the roommate was away doing a construction job.

Mark was always moving for one reason or other. He was a big hulk of a man who had played football in high school and liked to refer to himself as a "red-neck queer." His parents had made him move out of their house when they failed to turn him straight by threats and preaching.

I had been pissed off at Mark for trying to tell me how to run my life and being stingy with his dope, but now, in the spirit of Christian forgiveness, I called him on the phone and said, "Hey, how's it going, does Big'n have any more of that scotch?"

"The good scotch in the Harley Davidson decanter?" Mark asked in horror. "Helll, nahhh, I can't touch that! Big'n would kill me! I got some special diet pills if you need a pick-me-up…"

"Well, we can't do one without the other!" I barked. "Listen, man, this is no time to quibble over situational ethics! Pour the scotch in a cup and put some ice tea in the decanter to replace the scotch. You'll be moved or kicked out before they discover it's gone!"

Big'n and Fran were away at Bike Week in Daytona.

The next thing you know, my wife's cousin Mark and I are over at Big'n and Fran's house sharing a big Burger King cup full of good scotch. I thought I was ready to write, but Mark had other ideas.

"Oh, I see how it is," Mark started in on me. "Take my dope and then leave to go write that bogus crap you always write. Pushing your friends away! Chasing a dream!"

"But, the Sears plumber is supposed to show up at my house,"
I said.

Mark snorted in disgust, "Are you a dumb-ass or what?"

"What now, for God's sake?" I asked.

"You called Sears? You know they are a booj-wa outfit!"

He meant "bourgeois" and I don't even know if he knows what
it means. Or maybe he know what it means and just likes to say it
red-neck style on purpose, the way he says crick for creek and PO-
lice for the law.

I said, "What are you talking about, booj-wahh?"

"They take on more customers than they can possibly serve, just
to insure money coming in, but they don't give a rat's ass about you."

"Well," I said. "You may be right."

"I'm always right," he said smugly. "You know," he added, "They
came out with the last Sears catalog and I've got one. It'll be a
collector's item."

He waved the slick, glossy Sears catalog in the air. "Last one ever
made!" he said.

"Yeah, right," I said.

"Hey," Mark's face lit up. "I think we have a way to get revenge
on the Sears plumber. The empty haunted house across the street.
We call the plumber to that house, and nobody lives there so we can
do whatever we want!"

I said, "You mean, like, kick his ass?" I was just asking.

"And stuff pages of the Sears catalog up his ass!" Mark shrieked.

"Wait a minute," I cautioned firmly. "Nobody's gonna stick
nothing up anyone's ass!"

"You fuckin' closet poof," he yelled. "If we call the plumber to
the haunted house, we stuff pages up his ass! As long as he doesn't
see out faces, people will think the ghosts did it! See?"

"Fine," I said. "Whatever. And I'm not a closet poof. I just
happen to like drama, like you, but I'm not!"

"Yeah, yeah," he brushed me off.

By now it was 12 noon and we were buzzing. We drank deep from the cup of booze and Mark dialed the phone…

Someone at Sears answered the phone.

"Yes," Mark began. "I'm calling to ask why the plumber isn't here yet. Yes. My address is 2201 Blatbaum Place."

He was giving the address across the street.

"What?" he asked. "No. 2201. Yes. Well, I don't know why you have 2202 on your clee-up board. We're on the right side, about a mile from you as the crow flies…What? Crow. It don't matter, look, it's 2201 Blatbaum! Dammit, when can I expect someone?"

I had found a pack of Fran's Belle Air cigarettes, so I fired up one of those. I was rushing and feeling good but also worried about the passing of time. It was after one o'clock. More scotch.

The next thing I remember is, I'm in Big'n and Fran's bath tub in hot water and bubble bath, just wearing my underpants, reading an Easy Rider biker magazine I found.

Mark was in the kitchen cutting up vegetables to make a stew. He was stealing onions, potatoes, and carrots from the refrigerator, a can of Campbell's cream-of-something soup from the pantry. With wild abandon, he tossed smidgeons and dashes of every seasoning showcased in Fran's wall-mounted spice rack.

"I'm a witch!" he called out shrilly. "Bubble and brew, my cauldron stew!"

The damn Sears plumber van pulled up across the street. I was out of the bath and into a Japanese robe that belongs to Big'n & Fran's 19-year-old daughter, Stella, who was away at Flagler College in Saint Augustine. Mark and I gazed out the window at the plumber across the street.

"What are we gonna do?" I asked.

"Just follow my lead," Mark said authoritatively.

Much of the action is a blur in my mind but it involved a Sears plumber gagging and snorting as Mark hollered, "Squeal!" and pages and clothing were torn and some violent kicking and cussing and scotch flying all over the room. I know we forgot to remain anonymous.

I tried everything in my power to quell the atrocity, falling back by instinct on the "just say no" virtue.

I remember yelling at Mark, "He said no you perverted hick! What part of no do you not understand?!"

Mark always calls me a dumb ass but now he was dangerously out of control and risking jail time. I convinced Mark we had to flee the scene.

About 3:30 PM we were back at Big'n and Fran's house. I was starting to get paranoid because I knew my wife would be home in an hour or so. This was not at all the blissful 10:30 AM vibe; time was running out. Christmas was over and the toys were broken. Damn, now what?

I focused my eyes on the spoonful of soup Mark was holding in front of my face to taste. The soup was very good and it helped to clear my head.

"Where's the plumber?" I asked.

"Chasing a turd down desolation row!" Mark gleefully replied. "HeeHeeeee!"

I ate more soup to sober up and maybe hide my alcohol breath and then realized I was wearing the Japanese robe and some plastic deer antlers. Mark was now wearing a leather jacket he had found in a closet and a shower cap that belonged to Fran. I changed back into my clothes, throwing my wet underwear into the tank on the back of their toilet.

The glaring sun trounced upon my eyes when I walked outside and stumbled on the sandy grass lawn. I made my way home, put Visine in my eyes, and flopped down on the couch. When my wife came home, I pretended to be sick.

"Might be the flu," I said.

That night I told my wife, Sonya, "The stupid Sears plumber never showed up. I'm gonna cut my Sears card in two and mail it back to them."

"That's not what I heard," said Sonya. "While you were napping Mark told me the plumber showed up drunk across the street brandishing a pistol. Mark said he had to call the police and he thinks the plumber lost his job."

"Well, it serves him right," I said.

Part 2

Supernatural hauntings, Victorian drug use, and the strange disappearance of a Sears plumber – all these things swirled in my mind as I called my employer the next morning to say I was still "under the weather." I had a new idea for an article about drug use in the 19th century.

Across the street, the Florida haunted house loomed like a sinister pirate ship. It had a porthole window in which people reported seeing a strange figure looking out, the old rusted anchor in the front yard, and at the top of the dead coconut tree there perched a forlorn egret bird, like an omen.

My wife's cousin Mark, ex-Georgia football playing gay redneck, had done something in that house but I wasn't sure what.

Mark is an expert at redirecting blame and had convinced the police that the plumber was the guilty party for pulling a gun. We had not expected a gun.

The police came to my house around 9:00 AM to question me.

"I wouldn't know," I told them. "Plumbers are always missing when I call them. I heard he was drunk. Most of them drink on the job and rely on the sewage to cover the odor of booze."

I went inside and poured a generous dollop of MD-2020 wine into a coffee cup. I wanted to get this article about Victorian drug use started.

See, back in the day when people like Charles Dickens were alive, people could get medicine at the drug store that contained narcotics. I may have my time-line off here, but it wasn't long before Sigmund Freud was prescribing cocaine to help people get off the morphine. A buddy of mine who majored in psychology warned me not to slander the great psychoanalyst with "half-assed" accusations, saying that Freud later went back and told everyone that cocaine might not be such a good idea. He said it was more important to examine ours dreams for sexual objects and it's hard to dream if you are wide-awake, wired on blow.

The point is, aspirin is made from tree bark. How in hell did someone discover that? Somebody had such a bad headache they started gnawing on a tree? Many old witches were simply unlicensed pharmacists with an array of home remedies.

Nowadays, all I take is the occasional beer and, in the winter, Nyquil to slumber golden through the cold & flu bouts. Some cold medicines make me dream in color, complete movies from beginning to end, and if I could ever write those down, well, we'd really have something.

I was having trouble actually writing the article. I couldn't concentrate due to various minor aches and a general malaise in my brain, which needed clearing.

Strong black coffee helps, so I had some of that. Then, off to the store to buy cigarettes. The liquor store wasn't open yet so I picked up a bottle of strong, cheap wine, MD-2020, at the convenience store. I'm not trying to set a bad example for the young people, so don't drink in the morning. Unless you work all night; then I guess it would be okay.

Questions needed answers. What happened to the plumber? Of course, the place to start would be Mark, who had been directly involved in the melee.

I called Mark. He had convinced Big'n & Fran that while they were away at Bike Week, someone must have broken into their house while he was at work at the dry-cleaners. The culprit had cooked food and ransacked their daughter's wardrobe. They would not have understood that Mark and I had done this on a wild binge, bikers or not. Mark convinced them that they should not charge him any rent so he could work less often and stay home to guard the house. He assured them, "I won't tolerate the violation of your home," and they were grateful.

"Yeah," Mark told me on the phone. "I get off at noon and I need a ride home."

When I picked Mark up at the dry-cleaners I asked him, "What exactly happened to the plumber?"

"He was still in the house when we left," Mark said. "Hiding in a closet. He has been reported missing. When the police questioned me about it, hell yeah, I told them he has a gun. I told them I think he's schizophrenic because of his irrational behavior and that I'm quite worried about him."

"So," I asked, "Do you think he's still in the house?"

"I'm meeting him there today," Mark announced. "Perhaps you would like to come along."

"What? You're meeting him there?! What for?"

"You know," Mark explained, "How two guys can get in a fight and then be good friends, drinking buddies?"

"Go on," I said.

"Well," Mark continued, "After I tried to stuff a page from the Sears catalog up his ass, he had an epiphany of sorts, and confessed that as a plumber he was very disrespectful of his customers and he wanted to change. He said he didn't even want to be a plumber anymore and he's thinking about opening up a clinic to teach laymen how to fix their own pipes."

"You are a saint," I said earnestly. "So he's still in the house?"

"Yeah, and he still has at least three bullets in his gun," cautioned Mark. "We have to approach him carefully. He trusts me but he thinks you are two-faced. I told him I would keep you in check. By the way, his name is Kelp."

"Kelp?" I asked. "What the hell kind of a name is that?"

"He used to be a merchant seaman."

"That doesn't make any sense," I said.

~ **Intermission** ~

Cherub, the Red-assed Baboon

As kids, we were afraid to go into Mr. Claxton's yard. When a baseball or Frisbee went over his fence, it stayed there. That's because Mr. Claxton had an ugly baboon named Cherub, of all things, which was supposedly caged but our parents warned us that the hairy gargoyle might somehow escape, and those things can bite. And they are nasty, my Mom said. And my Dad said that one time when he was stationed overseas, a chimp had thrown shit at him.

We were out in my friend's yard one day and decided to put some dog excrement in a paper bag, and put the bag on someone's porch, set it in fire, and when they went to stomp out the fire, AHH, hahahaha, they soiled their shoe in the dog shit. This was something we always heard about other kids doing. We had never tried it but it was time, before we became teenagers and old enough for the courts to try us as adults. Of course, we were going to do this to Mr. Claxton even though we were afraid of Cherub, the red-assed baboon.

The three of us crouched behind some shrubs and peered into the dark, earthy-smelling wooden latticework door, which led under the fence into Mr. Claxton's yard. The door, about two feet square, was at the bottom of the fence was hidden by a row of shrubs. You could look in between the crisscrossed slat-boards into diamonds of night until our eyes adjusted to the dark, and we could make out Claxton's house in the distance.

Paul's older brother said if you go through that door, it's like a passage to another time, and all different times are like rooms in a mansion; you can go from one room to another. The old lady at the flea market had told Paul that there were zillions of "rooms" connected by doors, also called portals, and the rooms right next to each other looked almost exactly the same, like a movie frame, but if you travel to a distant room it will look different and you will be older or younger, or maybe dead. We weren't sure how heaven fit into it.

Cobwebs stretched as we pulled the door open. We looked at each other and then crawled, one by one, through the entrance, toward our adventure.

~ End of Intermission ~

Part 3

"That plumber is going to shoot us," I whined as we approached the 'haunted house.'

"Shoot you, maybe," Mark said. "You are the one who pissed him off. I saved him from a life of *greed*."

"Go drink some 'Cabana Boy' you Georgia fruit," I said to Mark. He hit me hard on the shoulder.

"Oww!"

As Mark and I strolled along the sidewalk toward the house, I felt a strange wave pass through me. I could tell Mark felt it, too, because he shuddered and shivered the same time I did.

"Whoa," I said. "Did you feel that?"

We reached the house and Mark tried the doorknob. It was unlocked. We walked in to an amazing sight.

The plumber had knocked out a large portion of the ceiling between the 1st & 2nd floor so you could look up, up all the way to a small hole in the roof, where beautiful hues of light cascaded down onto pipes. It was like a cathedral of pipes! Kelp the plumber had pipes running everywhere. Big pipes, small pipes, copper, steel, and white PVC plastic pipes, and a couple of black rubber-hose radiator pipes, and all these pipes stretched zigzag in all directions, from the floor up through the second floor to the ceiling. The pipes spread in all directions, turning at angles with elbow joints and connectors and clamps, and a few of the connections had small leaks and every few seconds we could hear the "drip/blip!" echo of water dripping onto the wet, carpeted floor. It was wild. The air was cool and relaxing. The plumber was nowhere in sight.

Silence in the house except for the "drip/blip!" of the water drops. It was several degrees cooler inside the house. Mark was wearing flip-flops so he waded right into the ankle-deep water. I hesitated because I was wearing my good Nikes, but I decided to follow him into the house.

We looked around in wonder at this monumental array of pipes. Sometimes we had to duck under or step over pipes to move through the room.

A noise came from inside a closet.

"Kelp?" said Mark. "Kelp, is that you in there?"

Something stirred behind the closet door.

I started to back away, remembering the gun.

Mark slowly turned the doorknob and opened the door a few inches.

"GAAAGGGGHHHHHHHH!!"

Something horrible, with hairy arms and legs flailing, burst out of the closet with an awful SCREECH!

Baboon!

Its ugly snarl of teeth and hate-filled eyes froze me. The ape grabbed Mark with one gnarly-knuckled hand on each of his shoulders and lunged forward, sinking its teeth into his neck. Mark fell backwards screaming.

"AHHHHHH! GET IT OFF ME!"

Mark and the baboon were thrashing in the water on the floor, the ape still biting his neck. I ran to them and kicked the ape on the side of the head. It raised up its fur-slathered head and looked at me.

Mark, being strong, threw the baboon off him and it rolled on the floor and stood up, that bow-legged ape-walk with both hands raised up over its head and came after me.

I don't know how I moved so fast, but as the baboon jumped at me, I held my hand outstretched, thumb tucked in tight, and rammed my hand and forearm into the beast's mouth and down its throat, in an effort to choke it. The baboon's sharp teeth closed on my forearm and I felt pain from the jerking of the animal's head. My only chance was to wrap my other arm around the ape's neck and pull it tight to my body to keep its head from thrashing. I held tight and stood up as straight as I could while the baboon's feet kicked me and kicked splashing water on the floor. I thought I was going to lose my grip.

"Over here!" Mark's shout echoed on the walls. "The closet!"

Mark held the closet door open with one hand while clutching his bloody neck with the other hand. There was blood spreading in the water.

I staggered with the baboon clumsily over to the closet. Mark grabbed the son-of-a-bitch's jaws, pried them off my arm, and we both threw the damn thing into the closet and slammed the door shut.

I was leaning on the door, breathing hard, my arm bleeding from the bite.

Mark fell to his knees with a thud and a splash, bleeding badly from the neck, crying and gasping through the tears, "Oh, God, Oh, God!" and was still holding his neck.

I yelled, "Mark, go outside! Go out the front door and I'll run out right behind you! You gotta slam the door shut as soon as I run out!"

"Okay, okay." He sobbed, standing up awkwardly, his big mass dripping water and blood. He staggered to the front door.

Mark walked out onto the front porch and stepped right on a flaming paper bag!

"OWW!" Mark cried as he lifted his right foot to his left hand, still clutching the bleeding neck trauma with his right hand, and suddenly there was shit everywhere from where his foot stepped on the bag.

"JESUS GAAAAA!" Mark wailed, hopping on one leg, bleeding, and slinging crap everywhere from his hand. He yelled, "MAMA!" and tumbled headlong off the porch into the front yard.

I noticed it was dark outside and three children were running, laughing in the distance toward some shrubs. I recognized this now as old Mr. Claxton's house.

From behind me, I heard the BANG of the closet door flying open and the baboon was bounding out again. This time it knocked me down, face down in the water, its pumping feet grinding my face against the rough, wet carpet, causing a big scrape on my forehead.

The ape bounded over me and out the front door, jumped over Mark, and was chasing the three running children. The kids looked back and screamed in terror. I was too weak to run after the baboon and Mark was wheezing hysterically.

The first child disappeared under the shrubs to safety, then the second child, but the vicious baboon snagged the third child with its teeth, right on the butt. The child screamed in pain and fear.

Suddenly out of nowhere, a dark figure of a man appeared in what looked like a one-piece jumpsuit. The light of the moon gleamed off the object in his hand – a big, heavy wrench.

Kelp the plumber swung the wrench hard and whacked the ape on the head. The baboon froze and then stood straight up, face to face with Kelp, with that bow-legged ape stance, both arms raised above its head. Then it fell forward with a thud, face down on the ground, and didn't move.

The third and last child, having been bitten, disappeared quickly beneath the shrubs through a secret door in the fence, and we could hear their footsteps echoing down the street as they ran.

We ran home as fast as our twelve-year-old legs would run. Which was pretty fast. I was so shook up I didn't notice I was leaving drops of blood in the road from the baboon's bite on my butt. Paul ran to his house and Mark ran to his grandmother's house where he was visiting from Georgia during summer vacation.

When I got home, my Dad was talking on the phone to Mr. Claxton.

"Don't worry, Claxton," my Dad was saying, "If I find out my boy was involved in this prank I'll…what?…Yes, I said prank. Look, a little shoe polish will…No, sir, no need to call the police! Like I say…"

"Oh, Lord!" my Mom cried when she saw me bleeding. "What happened?!"

"That *bamboon* bit me!"

My Dad stopped talking for a moment, looked at me, and said, "Goddammit, Claxton! Maybe I oughta sue your ass for lettin' that stinking ape bite my boy!"

Then Dad said to me, "I thought I told you to stay away from that son-of-a-bitch!"

Of course, Mom was all upset and started crying.

I figured my best defense was to cry, too. Mom inspected the wound and cleaned it with warm, soapy water and iodine, which hurt like hell and made my tears more genuine. She still wanted to take me to the emergency room.

"That thing might have rabies or God-knows-what," my Dad said.

I don't really know how the incident was resolved between Claxton and my parents. When you're a kid, things seem to blow over because your parents take care of it. I remember Claxton had some papers to prove the baboon had all its shots. I was grounded for a week and so were Mark and Paul.

I'll never forget Cherub, the red-assed baboon. I never even noticed if his ass was really red, but mine sure was for a while.

My wife, Mildra, thought it was crazy that two grown men could get into such a flap with a plumber and a baboon, but she was getting used to it.

The day after our ordeal, I met Mark and Kelp back in the weirdly piped house.

Kelp sat balanced on a horizontal pipe about six feet off the ground with a toothpick in his mouth. I was sitting on another pipe, which was low enough for my feet to touch the floor. Mark was leaning back in a folding chair with his feet propped up on still another pipe, smoking a cigarette. There were bandages on my arm and Mark's neck.

Over in the corner, sedated with animal tranquilizer but still awake, the baboon sat cross-legged on the floor with a plaster cast on the crown of its head, slowly and sloppily eating a Nutty Buddy ice cream cone. Kelp had adopted the animal and said he wanted to train it to operate a plunger.

Mark was explaining the time travel formula that we found bought at a flea market when we were kids.

"Picture a straight line," said Mark. "You are a dot in the middle of the line. If you travel forward to the right, you get older. Too far and you're dead. If you travel backward to the left, you get younger. Too far and you were never born. We think that might be Heaven but nobody knows for sure, and that's why we're afraid to die."

"Who do you think you are?" I asked. "Madeleine L'Engle?"

"Baby, I can rock a granny dress and a cane just as well as she can," Mark shot back. He continued, "Now, think of that straight line and join the ends together and you have a circle. Then, there is no longer a left or right."

Kelp spoke up excitedly, "It all blends together!"

I asked, "Does that mean Heaven can exist here on Earth?"

"So the theory goes," sighed Mark. "But a time travel formula from a flea market has its uncertainties."

The air was cool and soothing. The gentle "drip/blip" of water was relaxing. The thought of heaven on earth made me feel so good I stood up on the pipe and began to climb. Beautiful cascading hues of light filtered down from the hole in the ceiling as I started climbed the pipes like they were fantastic monkey bars on a secret playground.

I climbed without fear and felt such strength and calm and lack of pain, it was like I was a kid again, or almost like I was Superboy. I climbed to where the floor used to divide the first story from the second. I sidestepped over to another horizontal pipe and climbed higher. Getting wet didn't bother me. I was beyond the confines of 'wet'; I existed in bliss. Water doesn't hurt; it evaporates and all things are new.

I smiled and climbed until I reached the apex, the hole in the ceiling, which was bigger than it looked from down below. I stuck my head and shoulders up through the hole and could see all around, such a great expanse, so wide a world and safe, and I owned it all. I don't mean I owned it as if I could pick it up and take it; I owned it in the sense that it was all there for me and no one could take it away.

And miles and miles of clouds and earth and telephone lines and streets leading to oceans and sparkling oceans as far as the eye could see, and the swelling awe that engulfed me like looking at the biggest thing in the world. And as wide as the ocean was, I sensed it was also deep, so deep, and connecting everything.

Then I was standing on the roof with my arms outstretched and my head back and I felt a sudden jump in my stomach like when you dream you are falling. I realized I had been tense for so long and now the tightness in my stomach muscles relaxed and I noticed there were no aches or pains and my scalp tingled and I seemed to float as I laughed.

I fell back into the hole in the roof and remembered something Jack Kerouac said in the *Dharma Bums* about, "You can't fall off the side of a mountain," or something.

So I let myself fall. Rolling back into the hole I found myself gently supported by the network if pipes. Slowly, like a sloth, I rolled, slid, and melted down the pipe structure from one level down to the next. It seemed to take luxurious hours to settle on the first floor.

By this time, Mark was ready to leave. We said goodbye to Kelp and the baboon.

As we walked home, Mark said, "You know, the lady at the flea market said we would get our wish if we didn't fight time."

"That's right," I said. "And I did. I wanted to face that baboon again and I did it. What was your wish, Mark?"

"Well," said Mark, "When we were kids, hiding under those shrubs, it was like a secret hideout. I felt like I belonged. You know, I've lived from place to place ever since my parents disowned me."

"You're a nomad," I agreed.

Mark continued, "Kelp said I can move into that weird house with him. He knows someone at City Hall who fudged some papers so that the house doesn't exist on city records! It could be years before anyone finds out!"

"Years," I said. "Man, that could be all the time in the world."

I had used up all my sick days at work, so I had to buckle down and learn how to do my job. A few months later, my wife and I moved across town to live in a big house she inherited from her mother. Mark and Kelp still live in the "haunted" pipe house but I heard they had ditched the baboon in one of those big Salvation Army containers where people donate items by shoving them through a door flap. The idea was for the baboon to hand clothing and stuff out to Mark through the small door, but a cop car drove by and Mark hauled ass. A hysterical Salvation Army employee was in the news the next day but the ape got away. All the police found was a big, stuffed teddy bear and they assumed the employee was hallucinating and made him check into a clinic.

One day I'm going to make it back over to their house to catch up on my parallel existence.

Horizon of the Valley

Rickety wicker fellow,

Pocket watch and chain,

Tweed grouse hat,

Vest pocket holds celery.

He bends his elbow macaroni arm

To check the time,

Looks up, sees a purple swell of clouds.

Glow Sticks on Parade

Atoms in a steeple

Ladies in yellow dresses

Pouring iced tea.

Corduroy men catch baseballs.

Atoms mesmerize insects,

Insects in the steeple

Crucial daffodils,

Dry stalk daffodils,

Insects on parade.

Wavy lines coming out of the steeple,

Promenade around the corn stalks people!

For a feast of lights.

Glow Sticks on Parade.

Club Web

A vampire game rave club, The Club Web
Crowd chatters up a staircase, painted harlequins or corpselike
Wonders discussed dramatically from the drug effects
Sailor on two days leave, shook his head, you some fools.

He who winks trouble picture gallery
And effective blood human seduced and go
out into the curious crowd wise wicked entice consent a glass of
sherry
Master of Ceremony greets with a high shrill need.

No sex scene so dreamily erotic
Perfect, these remarks, he took him and opened a path
but to the hungry soul voice one knows special, indeed beautiful
the night
Into the office now, men looked back here, eyes cause trouble.

Go for a walk with me
The stone side-path and rich rooms connect
Sweet honeycomb buzzing, there are attractions circling
everything
Behind an arm and better wait who fools with wicked.

The stranger invited her, on all levels the fire began
he by by he he forward he but he he he loathes…
The townspeople surge onto the marble walk, look down,
satisfied it was not their soul,
Another wide-eyed pretty trickles cherry red.

The Euro Witches

Urban renewal efforts have transformed a shabby, long-neglected section of Jacksonville, Florida into the charming Piccadilly Circus Historic District, with freshly painted shops, bistros, faux Victorian lampposts of dark green, and a mosaic of paved stones aggrandizing the crosswalk. This is obviously not the "Piccadilly Circus" of London fame. It is a two-block area in Jacksonville, East of Five Points, West of Springfield, and South of Brooklyn. Tired of borrowing district nicknames from New York, the developers have looked to Europe for inspiration.

The Piccadilly Circus Open Mic Nights are held weekly in a former Morocco Temple building that bears a keystone engraved with the name of architect Henry John Klutho. Historians debate the connection between Klutho and this Morocco Temple, due to a persistent rumor that the keystone engraved with Klutho's name is actually his unkempt grave marker, stolen from Evergreen Cemetery and wedged over the front door between two stucco palm trees.

Three European devil worshipers, a woman and two men, visited this Piccadilly Circus of Jacksonville and somehow befriended me. I kind of regret it.

"Once, we were called aristocrats," said the bearded one with a twinkle in his eye. "Now they say Eurotrash!"

He laughed with his mouth closed, like, "Hhm, hmp, hmpf!" or something. I have trouble spelling laughs.

"You want to be in print?" asked the woman with a sexy

firmness. "You need an influencing power, an essence outside of yourself, a…"

"A muse?" I asked.

"No," she said, and looked at the bearded one, who in turn looked at the rotund, fleshy man who smirked and brushed a curl of hair from his forehead. It dropped right back down on his forehead again. He wore a cape, of all things. He called it his "opera house cloak."

"Do you believe in witchcraft?" asked the bearded man.

"I don't know," I said. "You mean, like, New Age, or cauldrons and black cats?"

"Hmp, hmp, humpf!"

Late that night, I went with the Euro-Witches to a Gothic church just off Piccadilly Circus. Don't misunderstand - this was not the "Piccadilly Circus" in London. It was a two-block area in Jacksonville, Florida - East of Five Points, West of Springfield, and South of Brooklyn, where some developers are creating a hip new place to shop and drink. Tired of borrowing the names of New York locations, the developers had looked abroad for inspiration.

The bearded man knelt and drew a pentagram on the floor with a piece of pastel blue colored chalk.

The fat man said, "Oh, look. Chalk like the little girls use for hopscotch."

The woman opened a bottle of champagne and poured four glasses.

The fat man produced a thermos from under the ample fabric of his cloak.

"This is for later," he said, placing the thermos on a dusty pew.

"A toast, then!" said the bearded man.

We raised our glasses of champagne.

"To gods and monsters, shrouds and veils, free your mind,

but guard your tails! Hmpf, hmpf, humf!"

We downed our glasses with one gulp.

The four of us stood in a circle around the pentagram and chanted incantations. I just moved my mouth and spoke low, half a beat behind the others, not knowing the words. We drank goat milk from the big man's thermos. Passed it around until it was empty. I didn't care for it. The firm lady's eyes rolled back in her head. Noxious air swirled over the pentagram like a wobbly trailer park tornado. Our skeletons turned sideways in our skin when the swirling miasma grew and spread until it encompassed our bodies and beyond, rushing out through broken windows into the dark city. Stray dogs rappelled down Klutho-designed high rises. One-way streets gave up trying. Doppler radar told weathermen to ditch their little brothers with granny. Activia introduced probiotic ectoplasm. Christopher Lee came back and signed a three-picture deal with Tim Burton. Old men's nose hair grew like time-lapse redwoods. A whistling room eloped with the giant floating head from *Zardoz*.

It was awful. Several days elapsed before I remembered my name and recovered my femur.

I have not seen the three Euro-Witches since that beastly experience, when the forces of howling insanity pitched a wang-dang-doodle all night long.

The Little Robot

Josh was taken away from his parents when they were arrested for political crimes. The young boy now lived in a world of confusion and loneliness.

At least he always had his plastic toy robot. It was a scale model of the robot from a television show called *Lost in Space*. His robot was his only friend.

The little boy's name was Josh.

Soon after arriving at the Agency, Josh got in trouble for having a rosary.

He only owned two things: the toy robot his father gave him and the rosary his mother gave him.

Children who had come to know their parents before being placed in the Agency were allowed two gifts. One gift from the mother and one from the father, or two from a single parent.

Josh's father was a robotics technician in a factory, so he gave the boy the eight inch toy robot with cool gadgets built in. For example, if you pushed a button on the robot's chest, a mechanical voice said, "Danger, danger, Will Robinson!" like on the TV show. The clear plastic bubble head, with radar gizmos inside, could be extended upward and pushed back down. Push a button on the robot's shoulder and its arm moved forward with its claw hand open. You could open a small plastic door on the robot's leg and see gears, or a picture of gears. Josh loved that robot and played with it all the time.

Josh's mother had given him a rosary. A small crucifix on a string with beads on it. You couldn't slide the beads up and down the string; each bead was sewed in place, immovable, equal distance from each other.   The Agency did not allow children to possess religious artifacts, but this one slipped through the cracks because Josh wore it around his neck with the cross under his shirt. His mother's idea and execution.

Josh's mother was not Catholic but it was her understanding that rosaries are used to teach or count prayers and recitations, so she made up her own system using the Lord's Prayer.

One of the Agency Administrators first caught Josh "praying his rosary." The boy held the first bead on the string between his thumb and forefinger and said, "Our Father." He held the second bead and said, "who art in Heaven." His fingers slid to the third bead, "Hallowed be Thy name." Next bead, "Thy kingdom come," and so on, each bead signaling the next word or phrase.

"What are you doing?" the big female nurse asked. She had sneaked up behind Josh. "What is that?"

Josh was unsure how to answer because of the tone of her voice.

He said, "Mom's rosary."

"Let me see that," demanded the nurse.

Josh held the rosary tight.

"Okay, then," said the big woman. "We'll see about this."

At the next staff meeting, she told the Head Administrator about the rosary.

The Head Administrator said, "Well, we can't have that. I don't really care personally, but we'll get a bad mark if it gets out, gets seen. Can we turn it into something else? Glue it to a board in the shape of a dinosaur?"

"I hardly see how," the nurse said, "His mother gave him the rosary. I'm afraid it might traumatize him if we take it away."

"I think *traumatized* is an exaggeration. Kids get upset," said the head man. "He'll outgrow it. Use some strategy. He seems to like that robot. That's much more appropriate for a young boy. It's scientific."

"It's a testament to man's accomplishments," said the nurse in a sarcastic voice, echoing his mentality. "I'll see what I can do."

One night after the lights went out, Josh pushed a button under his pillow and the robot blurted out, "Danger! Danger, Will Robinson!" and two younger children woke up crying in the room full of beds.

The big nurse came into the room.

"Give me that," she said.

Josh held the robot tight. The nurse got an idea.

"Let me borrow the robot for one night and I'll give it back tomorrow. That's a promise, and you know we always keep our promises."

Josh reluctantly handed the toy robot over to the nurse.

The next day, after breakfast, all the children were on their way to the library when the nurse pulled Josh aside.

"I'll make a deal with you," she told Josh. "I'll trade you the robot for the rosary."

"You promised it. Mom's rosary," stammered the boy. He was clutching the small cross in his pants pocket.

"Don't worry, I'll take good care of it," the nurse assured him in a comforting tone.

Still holding the crucifix in his pocket and trying to change the subject, the boy said, "Library. Library time."

The nurse reached into a big pocket on her white smock and brought out the robot. The boy's eyes opened wide. He held his hand out for the toy.

"Not until you give me the rosary," insisted the nurse.

Josh grudgingly produced the cross and beads from his pocket. The nurse put the robot in his other hand. He let go of the rosary and quickly held the robot in both hands.

A few days later, the Head Administrator was in a good mood. He told the nurse, "I'm very happy with the progress Josh has made. He shows a lot of potential with hands-on skills. I saw him taking that toy robot apart and putting it back together."

Josh had disconnected the little speaker inside the mechanical man. That way he wouldn't accidentally push the button and make people upset with the robot's loud voice.

Josh had discovered that no one could tell what he was thinking, which was a relief to him. He pretended to hear the robot speaking, but in his head. He found he could imagine the robot saying whatever he wanted.

The next day the Head Administrator watched Josh from a distance. The boy was quietly engrossed in playing with the robot's many gadgets. He seemed to have forgotten the rosary. The Head Administrator felt pride and a sense of accomplishment for leading the boy away from superstition and toward a practical, scientific pass-time. He smiled a satisfied smile.

What the Administrators didn't know was that, as the boy played intently with the robot, this was happening in stealthy secret:

When Josh clicked the button on the robot's chest, he thought silently, "Our Father." Then he extended the clear bubble-like head upwards and thought, "Who art in Heaven," He clicked the arm spring button and thought, "Hallowed be Thy name." Clicked open the small plastic door on the robot's leg, "They will be done." click, "Forgive us our sins" click, "as we forgive others..." click

Until he fell asleep.

Synapse

The two medics had to shield their eyes from the glaring light when they looked up at me. Wishing to avert the helicopter searchlight away from the them, my hands fumbled for the navigation stick in the pitch dark cockpit. The medics bravely crouched over an injured body on the ground, trying to do their job, even as I nose-dived toward them against my will. I blinked and looked away. Then the treetops lit up and I was sailing upwards, toward the woods.

I remember bright green pine needles casting jet-black shadows from the intense light. The pine needles hissed and shriveled from the heat as I swooped up through a cloud of steam and emerged to see stars and a silver crescent moon. The moon crescent turned sideways and shot upward, but it was really me turning sideways and falling. The grass lit up and I felt the hard, hard ground jarring me unconscious.

I thought I saw the medics bending over me.

I woke up in a hospital bed. No broken bones, but feeling bruised all over, with some bandages on my arms and head.

"Out of body experiences," said Dr. Gray. "I've had people tell me they saw themselves laying on the operating room table." He pointed to the side of his head with the stem of his unlit pipe and said, "The mind is remarkable."

Dr. Gray put the pipe back in his mouth long enough to scribble something on a clipboard.

"Your pipe isn't lit," I said.

"Helps me to not smoke," he answered.

"If I wasn't the pilot, who was?" I asked the doctor.

"There's a good chance your memory will return, Lieutenant Dassett," Dr. Gray assured me. "I told the legal team they will have to wait before asking you any more questions. They haven't accused you of killing the two medics. They just want to find out what happened."

"*I* want to find out what happened!" I moaned.

"Well," said Dr. Gray, "You obviously weren't flying the helicopter, because it was nowhere to be found. You either jumped or fell out of the cockpit before the pilot flew away."

"How long before I can get out of here?" I asked.

Dr. Gray said, "Your orders are to not talk about this to anyone. For security reasons. And even if you start feeling better, don't be too anxious to leave. You are under orders not to leave the hospital."

"Doctor's orders?" I asked.

Dr. Gray thought for a moment before removing the pipe from his mouth again.

"Yes," he said. "And Captain's orders as well."

I rested my head back on the pillow, looked around the room, and closed my eyes.

Later, having no TV in my room to distract me, I thought back to the day I first met the two researchers who would conduct the experiment I had volunteered for. Bob Vereen and Alice Smith were not in the military, but they had a military contract and worked in a lab on the base. Their laboratory building was only a short walk from the hospital where I was now a patient.

I remembered the three of us sitting casually in Dr. Bob Vereen's office. Smiling Bob, in his mid-thirties, wore his usual short sleeve dress shirt and tie, his stomach hanging slightly over his belt. He was always pulling up his slacks because they inched down under his gut when he tried to hold it in. He liked to slip off his brown loafers when relaxing with his feet up on the desk. The other researcher was Dr. Alice Smith. Attractive, nice, younger and more physically fit than Bob, but more formal and professional, Alice always wore her white lab coat.

Bob had once remarked to me, "If you think she looks good in that lab coat, you should see her in a bathing suit."

"I bet so," I laughed, "Is she married or what?"

"No," said Doctor Bob. "She's single. Don't bring this up to her, that we talked about her. She's still friends with my ex-wife."

So, we sat in the office, Bob and I drinking coffee, Alice drinking bottled water.

"Well, what kind of guinea pig am I going to be?" I asked them. "You're not going to dose me with LSD and watch me wig out, are you?"

Smiling Bob laughed, "No, sorry. You wish."

Alice said, "We're working on ways to help people who are paralyzed, Lieutenant Dassett. Mostly war casualties. You fit the criteria because of your left hand. What do you hope to get out of this?"

I looked at my stiff hand and said, "I want to fly again."

Bob said, "You were a helicopter pilot, I understand."

"I was, until I was grounded. I mean, I think I can fly with one good hand but regulations say otherwise.

Doctor Bob pulled something out of his desk drawer and chuckled, "Check out what I made."

It looked like a disposable camera that he had taken apart and lashed back together with black electrical tape, with two big silver nail heads sticking out of the top.

Bob said to me, "Alright, test subject. Let me test this on you."

"Oh, for God's sake, Bob," said Alice. "Don't listen to him, Lieutenant. It's one of his home-made toys."

"Is that a Taser?" I asked.

"Sure is," said Bob. "Made it myself. This little bastard will knock you on your ass!"

I asked, "You mean a disposable camera has that much power?"

"Nah," he said. "I kicked it up a few notches. I installed a couple of little step-up transformers. They take the juice from the battery, bat it back & forth a few thousand times and store the charge in a capacitor."

Bob stood up and walked toward me. "When these two nail heads come in contact with you, and I push this button here…"

"Get that thing away from me," I said, backing up.

"Come on, Dassett, there's no permanent damage."

I decided to stand my ground.

"I will put that thing up your ass," I said.

Bob stopped and laughed, "Ah, man, I'm just kiddin' with ya."

Alice said, "It's not funny, Bob."

Bob pulled his belt and waistband up over his gut, sat on the front edge of his desk, and said, "I would like to try it somebody, though."

I said, "Why don't you try it on yourself?"

Bob chuckled.

Alice said, "Well, this isn't a good way to start off with our volunteer. Put it away, Bob."

"These experiments," I asked. "Are they going to hurt?"

"Not at all," said Alice. "We'll use a local anesthetic on your scalp, and the brain itself actually feels no pain."

Now I'm laying in a hospital bed wondering if Doctors Bob and Alice will have to find another guinea pig. "If so," I mused, "maybe it's for the best. I don't much like smart-ass smiling Bob."

The next day I was able to walk out to a sunny little outdoor rest area; a patio with tables and chairs. It was still part of the hospital, so I figured it was within the limits of my orders. I sat at a round concrete table, shielded from the sun by an umbrella on a pole in the center of the table. An elderly man and woman sat at another table over on the other side of the patio, talking quietly.

I sensed someone looking at me and turned to see a short young man standing to my right. He was apparently a patient, wearing a white robe and slippers, smoking a cigarette.

"Lieutenant Dassett?" he asked meekly.

"Yep, that's me," I said.

"Can I sit down?"

"Be my guest."

He sat down opposite me at the table, leaned forward, and almost whispered, "They don't want me to talk to you but I think I should."

I was prepared to say nothing. He might be gathering information for who-knows-what and I was under orders not to talk.

I said, "I really don't feel like talking."

"Look," he said, still speaking low, "I know you didn't steal any weapons."

I just looked at him. What did he mean, "steal any weapons?"

"I'm on your side," he said nervously.

"Well," I finally said, "I certainly haven't stolen anything. Are you okay? You seem kind of shaky."

The young man took a long drag on his cigarette, held the smoke for a moment, then looked up and blew the smoke toward the umbrella. The smoke curled and floated over onto me.

I felt strange. The smoke must have triggered a flashback. The night sky. The burning pine needles. I spaced out and forgot about the kid sitting next to me. I must have been staring into space.

"Lieutenant!"

"Huh? Oh, sorry. What?"

"Are you remembering something?"

"No."

"Look," the kid said, "I know you didn't burn those guys."

"Burn?" I asked.

The young man continued, "Aren't they charging you with stealing a helicopter and some incendiary bombs?"

I didn't say anything but my mind was racing, trying to put this together. I had no memory of stealing anything but I remembered diving on the medics and their patient. My curiosity struggled with my discipline. I felt like I had a right to know some things.

I asked, "Are you the guy that was lying on the ground?"

"What?" asked the young man.

"With the medics," I said. "The medics were kneeling over someone on the ground. Was that you?"

Now it was the young man's turn to stare. The long ash of his cigarette fell onto the table.

"There was no patient other than you," he said. "They were kneeling over you."

"No," I said. "Before that. I saw them bending over someone else before I fell.

"There was nobody else," he said again. "Those two medics had no other patient but you."

We looked at each other, both puzzled.

"Then who got burned?" I asked. "You said somebody was burned."

"The two medics," he said incredulously. "You didn't know? They were burned to death by some kind of incendiary device. Or something."

I was getting more worried and confused by the minute. This was a lot more serious that stealing a helicopter, an act which I was apparently a party to. I seriously wondered for a moment if I had gotten drunk out of my head again and done something terrible.

"Have they found the helicopter?" I finally asked.

"No helicopters are missing," said the young man. "Inventory shows them all accounted for and," he lit another cigarette, "there is no evidence that any unauthorized flight took place."

"How do you know all this?" I asked.

"I wasn't supposed to be there that night."

"Where?"

"The lab building. Where they were testing. I was down the hall using one of the computers. I wasn't supposed to be there. I think Dr. Vereen and Dr. Smith know what happened."

"Bob and Alice?" I pondered out loud.

I remembered that behind the lab building is a lawn. Beyond the lawn are some woods. Pine trees. We had squadron picnics out there sometimes. Is that where I saw the two medics?

The young man said, "Nobody knows what I saw. I'm not even sure what I saw."

"Who are you?" I finally asked.

"Pratt. Private Pratt, at least until I get my discharge. I'm hoping to get out of the service, be a civilian again, leave here and never come back. That's why I don't want any trouble."

"Why are you here?" I asked

"To help you."

"No, I mean, why are you in the hospital?"

"I'm in the psych ward," he said sheepishly.

"Oh, great. Are you crazy?"

"I don't think so."

"You don't think so."

Private Pratt fumbled in his robe pocket and pulled out a folded newspaper clipping.

"Here," he said. "Take this and read it when no one is around. I've got to go."

I took the paper and watched Pratt walk away.

Back in my room, I unfolded the section of newspaper. Pratt had drawn a red square around an article. With the same red marker, he had scrawled the four digit phone number to his hospital room in the margin. The article said:

> Shelly Vereen, President of Vereen Children's Mentoring Program, was found dead in her Garden Heights home today around 9:00 am. According to police, her badly burned body was discovered in bed by her fiancé. There are some unusual circumstances surrounding Ms. Vereen's death. According to police, only her bed and body were burned. The rest of the room was unharmed other than a window which was broken from the outside, leaving glass inside the room. An investigation is ongoing. Shelly Vereen is the ex-wife of Dr. Bob Vereen, who is scheduled to appear at a fund-raiser for medical research to help victims of paralysis. At this time, it is not known if Dr. Vereen will cancel his appearance. He could not be reached for comment.

I lay in my hospital bed and read the article twice, more slowly the second time. Why did Pratt give me this? Bob Vereen. "Smiling Bob" as I called him. One of the researchers I had been assigned to. His ex-wife killed in a fire.

My head hurt. I touched the top of my head and felt the bandage with a twinge of pain. Tired of my scalp sweating under the bandages, I pulled them off. Gently touching a shaved spot on top of my head, it felt like a hard baseball stitch. I looked at my fingers. No blood. Must be healing.

When the nurse came, I hid the newspaper under my pillow. She put another bandage on my head and gave me two pills.

"This one is for pain," she said. "And this one will help you relax so you can sleep."

I pretended to take the pills and the nurse left the room.

Later that night I was restless. I got out of bed and slowly opened the door a couple of inches. I saw no one in the hall so I slipped out for a walk, avoiding the nurse's station, which was around the corner. Two doors down, through an open door, a TV was yakking.

"Gala affair tonight…" said the TV announcer, "Overshadowed by tragedy. Dr. Vereen *is* expected to attend, saying his ex-wife would want it that way."

I stood outside the room, where the occupant couldn't see me, watching the television. So Dr. Bob's big benefit was tonight and they've decided not to cancel it.

"Crazy," I thought.

Should I walk out of this hospital and find civilian clothes and attend this friggin' gala? That would be the stupid thing to do.

Except, sometimes I do stupid things. Did you know my hand isn't really paralyzed? Yeah, I had faked them into grounding me before they found out my real secret. Sometimes I had tremors it was so bad. When I tried to stop drinking. I didn't want to admit that. So I had this medic who owed me a favor inject Lidocaine into my left hand, with a tourniquet applied to the wrist for two minutes to keep most of the numbness in my hand. This wouldn't fool the doctors forever, but it was a way to stall for time while I tapered off my drinking, or so I thought.

I returned to my room and paced back & Forth, wanting a drink. Having not taken my medication, I was restless. I decided to go to the benefit, have a few drinks, and see what Dr. Bob is up to.

I called Private Pratts's room and he answered before the first ring ended. I told him what I wanted to do, but I didn't know how I was going to sneak past the nurse's station. Besides the nurses, there was a security guard who walked around and usually sat in the nurse's station when he wasn't making his rounds, but he kept his eyes open.

Pratt whispered on the phone, "Did they post a guard at your door?"

"No," I said. "There's just the regular security guard who walks around."

"Amazing," Pratt said. "Just the one guy?"

"Well, they think I'm doped up," I explained. "And besides, they think I'm afraid to disobey orders not to leave."

Pratt whispered excitedly, "I've got it all figured out. That guard is mainly looking for people in hospital gowns and robes. There's a Captain up here in the mental ward strapped to a bed in his underwear with the D.T.'s. They've got his uniform neatly hanging in the closet. He's not going anywhere."

"Go on," I said.

"I believe his uniform will fit you. The staff lets me walk around because I've never tried to leave, so I can bring you the uniform. We can walk right by the nurse's station."

"I don't know," I said. "They still might recognize me."

"No," said Pratt hoarsely whispering. "You walk with your head turned toward me. I'll be on your left in my hospital gown, the nurse's station will be over to our right. I'll be talking to you, so you have a reason to be looking at me. You don't say anything. It's just a short walk to the elevator or the stairs."

"These elevators always take so long to come," I protested. "They'll say something to us."

"Okay, listen. While you're looking at me, I'll say, 'Captain, I get nervous in elevators. Can we take the stairs up to my room?' They might wonder about us, but they won't put it together that fast. For all they know, you're my Squadron Captain come to visit me. They're always telling me to go to my room before curfew, so they'll think, 'Okay, Pratt's going up to his room and he's with a Captain, so we don't have to worry about him.' We'll walk through the door to the stairs. But we don't go up. We haul ass down the stairs to the first floor. Even if the guard decides to follow us, he'll be going up, not down, see? You can slip out and call a cab. I'll go on back to my room."

"Is there a hat?" I asked.

"Oh, yeah. Hat, shoes, medals, a whole Captain's uniform!"

"You don't want to escape, too?" I asked.

"Hell, no," he said. "Not like that. I'm still trying for my discharge papers."

"Well, come on, then," I said.

"A new guard comes on duty at 7:00 PM," he said. "I'll be there a few minutes after that."

The whole idea was stupid, but my craving for a drink of the hard stuff overruled my good sense.

Private Pratt was at my door a few minutes later. He had a big paper bag from the hospital gift shop. Inside the bag was the uniform. He said the guard had spoken to him as he walked by the station. He told the guard that his Captain was visiting someone down the hall and he was going to drop in on them, too.

We walked by the guard and nurses just as planned. I took a cab to a nearby bar where the owner is a friend of mine. I left the Captain's hat and jacket in the cab and asked the driver to wait. My bar-owner friend leant me money and gave me three shots of Jack Daniels. What a guy!

I took the cab to the ritzy Hawkshore Hotel where the upscale fund-raising affair was in full swing.

"I'm a patron," I told the doorman, and removed my hat as I walked in wearing the Captain's uniform.

Men in tuxedoes and women in evening gowns filled the ballroom. The speeches were over by this time. Hotel staff navigated trays of hors d'oeuvres and glasses of champagne from guest to guest. I accepted a glass of champagne and walked among the crowd, looking for Alice Smith or Bob Vereen, feeling bold from the alcohol. A pianist played soft dinner music.

There they were! Through a set of open doors, together on a balcony, Doctors Alice and Bob were talking under the night stars. For once she wasn't wearing her lab coat. In formal attire she was elegantly good looking. They didn't see me as I approached. I stood over to the side of the entrance.

Dr. Bob was saying, "What's the matter? Relax!"

He was holding her arm but she jerked it briskly from his grip and looked away from him.

"Don't put your hands on me again," she said.

"I don't see the big deal. Let's enjoy the evening!" Bob said. His voice sounded a bit drunk.

Alice said, "I think we had better keep this relationship professional, Bob."

"If that's what you want," Bob said sarcastically. "And after I gave you such a good evaluation!"

"You damn well better be joking," said Alice. "And it's not funny. Stop it!"

When she yelled 'stop it' I had to see what was going on. I gulped down the champagne in my glass and walked out onto the balcony.

Bob was gripping Alice's forearms, and she was struggling to pull away from him. They both looked at me.

Bob relaxed his grip on Alice and said to me, "What the hell are you doing here?"

Alice said, "Lieutenant Dassett! I thought you were in the hospital."

I asked, "What the hell is wrong with you, Bob?"

Bob's arms dropped to his sides.

"None of your business, asshole!" he replied. "And what are you doing in a Captain's uniform?"

I jammed the hat back onto my head defiantly.

Alice, arms loosely crossed, was rubbing her forearms gently with her hands, where Bob had gripped her.

"I've got to go," she said.

Bob started to follow her but I put my arm out in front of him. I actually wanted to go with Alice, to ask her about everything that had happened, to make some sense of the two burned medics and all the rest. But it was clear Bob would follow her, too.

As Alice walked back into the ballroom , Bob and I squared off on the balcony. We were both feeling the booze.

"You dick!" said Bob. "Get out of my way!"

"You're the dick!" I countered.

"Oh," he said, slurring his words, "That was a *cleffer* come-back."

Bob hiked up his pants as he always does, picked up a half-full cocktail glass from the balcony railing, and quickly drank the contents of the glass. He leered at me drunkenly.

"You," he pointed a finger at me with the hand still holding the empty glass, "Are AWOL, I suspect."

"Don't you worry about that, fat boy," I said.

He shoved past me.

"Where do you think you're going?" I asked.

"I'm going to catch up with Alice after I report you to security."

"You stay away from her!" I yelled

"Don't tell me what to do, Lieutenant. I can go anywhere I want." He brought his drunken sneer close to my face, and said in a low, twisted voice, "I can go places nobody else can go. I'm an incubus."

"What?" I asked.

"You are an incubus, too, Lieutenant Dassett. "A stupid one. No, worse than that! You are an angel of death! Security!"

He raised the hand holding the glass and motioned for someone.

"Security!"

A tall, fit man in a dark suit and an earpiece in his ear quickly approached. I didn't know if he was military, secret service, or hotel security, but I knew Bob was going to turn me in for leaving the hospital against orders and impersonating a Captain. I grabbed Bob by the lapels of his tuxedo and shoved him at the security man as hard as I could.

As he stumbled against the tall man, Bob leaned forward and I saw something strange on the top of his head. Strands of his combed-over hair fell loosely out of place, revealing a small raised implant in his scalp.

I froze, trying to recapture a vague memory.

I took off my hat and felt the top of my own head, where a strip of white tape held a piece of gauze in place. I pulled off the gauze and felt again. Right in the middle of the stitches on top of my head was a small dimple in the skin. Something had been removed and stitched up.

The security guy must have seen the look on my face because he just stood there for a moment, wondering what the hell was wrong. Dr. Bob was back on his feet, reaching into his jacket pocket.

"I'm telling you," Bob yelled as he pulled the Taser from his pocket, "This man should be placed under arrest!"

Bob rammed his homemade Taser against my chest.

Spasms of pain paralyzed my lungs from breathing. Searing high voltage, like angry fire ants, made me jerk involuntarily. But with the shock came the flowing restoration of my memory. I knew the truth even as I slumped onto the floor and lost consciousness.

In my dream, I was back in the laboratory, the night the medics were killed. Bob and Alice were prepping me for the test.

"That didn't hurt much, did it," Alice Smith had said, as the pulled the syringe needle out of my scalp.

Feeling comfortable in a kind of dentist's chair, I said, "No. You're pretty good at that, I'm happy to say. Now what?"

"Well," said Alice, "As you see on this chart, information travels in the brain from one neuron to the other."

The chart showed a diagram of the brain, and inside the brain were a bunch of dots. Some of the dots were connected by little lightning bolt symbols.

"These dots represent neurons," Alice said, "And information is carried from one dot to the other by *synapses*. Most brain synapses are chemical, but a small percent of them are electrical."

"I've got electricity in my brain?" I asked.

"Everyone does," she said. "Very low voltage. That's why, in order for a brain synapse to have any effect on an outside object , like an artificial limb, we have to amplify the electrical charge many times over, using capacitors and step-up transformers."

They had implanted a little plug-in socket in the top of my head, where they could attach a wire, which would make contact with the synapses in my brain and carry them to an amplifying device. I stayed awake through it all, until something went wrong. I remember a big ball of lightning crackling as it rose to the ceiling and caught the room on fire. I remember Alice looking down at me.

"He's not breathing, Bob," she had said. "I don't think his heart is beating!"

Bob had called in the two medics to resuscitate me. The medics carried me outside because of the fire in the room. Bob had a fire extinguisher, blowing white foam all over the place.

Outside, looking down, I saw myself on the ground with the medics bending over me. The medics looked up and saw the same car-sized ball of lightning that had started the fire inside. It had crashed through a window and was now diving on them. There was no helicopter. That was my body on the ground and my highly amplified brain plasma pulsating overhead. I didn't want to dive on them. I veered off, into the pine trees, my mutant synapse showering a trail of sparks, then upward, and vanished in a cloud of acrid smoke, like a burned-out sun.

But I had pulled back too late to save the medics. Their heads and upper bodies were fatally burned. I had only succeeded in saving myself.

I think I screamed in my sleep.

"Lieutenant Dasset."

Eyes closed. I hear a familiar whisper.

"Lieutenant Dassett."

I opened my eyes and there was Private Pratt, standing near me, whispering. I couldn't move my arms and legs. I was strapped to a hospital bed. I looked at Pratt.

"How do you feel, Lieutenant?"

"How is it that you can walk around this hospital anywhere you want?" I asked Pratt weakly.

"You're up here in the psych ward now," he said. "With me. They don't know that I know you. I can't talk long, they'll be back soon."

"What's an incubus?" I asked.

"An incubus?"

"Bob Vereen said he was an incubus."

"It's an old superstition," Pratt said. "Like goblins and ghosts."

"Why would he say that?"

Pratt said, "An incubus is like an evil spirit that floats into a woman's bedroom at night to, you know, have sex with her. There's the succubus, which is female, and the incubus, which is male."

"Shelly Vereen's window was broken when she was burned to death in her bed," I said, alarmed.

"Yeah," said Pratt.

"Alice Smith is in trouble," I said, struggling at the straps that held me. "What day is it?"

"Not so loud," whispered Private Pratt intently. "What's the matter?"

"Vereen's going to kill Alice Smith if he hasn't already! God! Get these straps off me! Come on, get 'em off!"

"I can't. This time they have a military guard posted outside the door and the regular security guard. What do you mean, 'kill Alice Smith?' What…"

"He'll burn her! The same way he burned his ex-wife! What day is it?" I demanded.

"It's only the day after you snuck out. Calm down," Pratt said. "They brought you back in here last night."

"Pratt," I tried to lower my voice and regain my calm. "Pratt, listen to me. You're the one that brought me the newspaper article. You must know something. Put it together, for God's sake!"

"Did Dr. Vereen burn those two medics?" asked Pratt.

"No, no, I…I…I didn't mean for them to be hurt…I…"

"I saw the fireball," said Pratt. "The night it happened. It almost got you, too. The medics shielded you there on the ground. That's why I knew you didn't do it. I didn't want to get involved at first because I have problems of my own. I'm just trying to get out of the military and don't want to rock the boat. So what are you saying happened?"

"Just get me loose!" I pleaded. "Jesus Christ, I don't have time to explain the whole fucking thing!"

Pratt was backing up, getting ready to leave. The military guard, followed by a nurse and an attendant entered the room.

"What's the problem?" asked the nurse.

"Why am I strapped down?!" I demanded. "Where's Dr. Smith, Dr. Alice Smith, where is she?"

"You are no longer assigned to her," the nurse said calmly.

"That doesn't matter!" I shouted. "Where is she? Is she here today? Dr. Vereen is going to kill her!"

They looked at me like I was a raving maniac.

The nurse said, "I'm going to give you something to calm you down."

I protested in vain as she slid the hypodermic needle into my arm. I overheard the attendant say in a low voice, "Should we reschedule the shock therapy?"

"No," the nurse answered. "We'll proceed."

I remember being wheeled down the hall and into another room. Other people stood around me. They placed a rubber tooth-guard in my mouth so I wouldn't bite my tongue or chip my teeth. I wanted to speak but only gibberish came out.

Why are they doing this? Are they trying to help me or hurt me? Did Bob Vereen order this? Do they think I'm crazy? Did they find out I'm an alcoholic? Am I really losing my mind?

Racking pain! The shock therapy was in session.

My eyes were closed and I felt relaxed. The painful shocks were fading. I could see the doctors and attendants. I could see the tops of their heads. I saw myself lying on the stretcher. I was doing it again. This time there was no fireball of lightning. The shock treatment was opening up my own mind's ability to travel.

I saw the window in the shock therapy room, then the window ledge, then outside. The street. Brick walls of buildings. Trees. The street below. It was a beautiful feeling. No pain. Sailing over the roads. A church steeple. A bank. Sailing past telephone poles, following telephone lines. A bird lands on top of a stop sign and my trail somehow catches the bird's eye; it's head flicks left to right as it watches my winding progress around the corner and further on. A bus rolls to a stop at a red light but I keep moving. Sailing.

Alice Smith lives in the sandstone brick apartments up ahead.

As I approach the apartment building, two police cars and an evidence van are parked below me. Yellow tape is blocking off the area.

I can already see the shattered window to Alice Smith's apartment, surrounded by black soot on the tan brick.

I fly in through the window. Alice's bedroom. One of the policemen has a camera.

Soot on the wall over the headboard where a picture hangs, glass cracked from the heat and the canvas scorched brown, picture obscured.

The bed, a sunken, smoldering pit of horror. The charred skeletal remains of Alice Smith in the sagging remains of the mattress.

I didn't want to see any more. I tried to close my eyes but there was no shutting out the scene. Then I remembered, my eyes were already closed.

Of all things, I remembered reading something about out-of-body experiences by Carlos Castaneda. The old Indian teacher had said, "When you want to return to your body, look at your hands." With a great effort, I opened my eyes wide. I craned my neck and head forward and saw my hands down by my sides, struggling against leather straps. I relaxed my neck, let my head drop back onto a soft pillow, and saw the white ceiling of the hospital room. I was back.

Days passed. I slept a lot. I could barely lift food to my mouth. They stuck an intravenous tube in my arm. The restraints were removed.

One day I opened my eyes to see Dr. Gray holding that empty pipe in his teeth, looking at my chart.

He removed the pipe from his mouth and said, "Remember me?"

"You're the first doctor I spoke to after the two medics were killed," I said.

"Well, your recent memory is okay," he observed. "And your hand," he remarked with a suspicious smile, " seems a lot better."

"Yeah," I mumbled weakly.

Dr. Gray continued, "Do you remember me telling you that I had asked the legal team to leave you alone for a while?"

"Yeah."

"Well, they're back and they really want to talk to you soon. Do you feel up to it?"

My mind was racing. I had no way of knowing what influence Bob Vereen had over my treatment here, or if he was a friend of Dr. Gray. As long as I was a patient, especially a mental patient, it seemed that Vereen had some power over my situation.

"Are the police here now?"

"No," said Dr. Gray. "They want me to call them when you're ready to talk to them."

"I want to go to the police station," I said.

Dr. Gray said, "There's no need for that. They're willing to come here."

"No," I said. "I will talk to them at the police station or not at all."

"Well, I don't understand, but, I'll tell them. They can probably be here first thing in the morning to pick you up. They are going to want to escort you there, of course."

"Sure," I said. "That's fine."

Alone in my room that night, I mulled over the situation. Bob Vereen probably thought nobody would believe me about any of this. I'm in the crazy ward, after all.

On the other hand, why would he take the chance? I could lead the authorities to his brain synapse amplifying apparatus if they did listen to me. I didn't think Dr. Bob wanted me to make it to the police station tomorrow. I was sure he could check on me anytime and find out I was going to the police. I was convinced that if I waited until morning, Bob would come for me this night.

I did the old trick, pillows-under-the-sheets, to make it look like I was in bed asleep. First I sat in the corner of the room and waited. Then I thought of the whole room being lit up by one of Bob's giant, bloated brain sparks, so I hid in the bathroom with the light out. I waited.

Just after midnight I heard a squeaking, squeegee sound. It was the windowpane, shivering at a growing onslaught of evil dragon's breath. The crash of breaking glass! The loud, harsh pop and hum of electricity. A rectangle of bright, thin rays of light around the edges of the bathroom door.

The guard outside my room heard the noise, opened the door, and looked in.

He said, "Holy shit! Get a fire extinguisher!"

The regular night security guard said, "Here! What's going on?"

I barely opened the bathroom door and peeked out. One guard was spraying CO2 from the fire extinguisher all over the flaming bed while the other guard looked on. They both had their backs to me.

One guard shouted, "Lieutenant Dasset!"

The other guard asked, "Is he there? Is that him in bed?"

But Bob had failed at burning me to death in bed.

I bolted out of the bathroom, behind the two guards, out the door into the hallway, in pajamas and bare feet. I sprinted as fast as I could past the nurse's station, into the stairwell, and was barreling down the steps three at a time. I fell once, rolled down a few stairs, jumped up, and kept on running. Down to the first floor and out the door.

I ran along the sidewalk, around the corner of the hospital, and toward the lab building.

The front door to the lab building was locked. The side door was also locked. I picked up a trash can and hurled it through a closed window. Quickly chipping away the jagged shards of glass with the trash can lid, I climbed into the lab building.

Looking around the dark room, I wondered if Bob had heard the breaking glass. Was he still weak or unconscious from the effects of sending out his murderous thoughts? If I could find him like that, it would be like finding Dracula asleep in his coffin. I walked across the room and found a door that led into the hallway.

As soon had I entered the hallway I heard a noise behind me. Dr. Bob, fully conscious, lunged at me with the Taser.

My anger boiled. I grabbed Bob's throat with both hands, but his Taser sent spasms of pain into my stomach, wrenching my gut tight from the high voltage. My vision went blurred and then dark.

All I wanted was to escape. How could all this have happened? Why? Not so long ago, everything was good. The spring and summer were so nice here. I could see the water fountain in the middle of the courtyard. I floated over the fountain, over the tops of buildings, a basketball court. Down there is a young couple sitting together on a bench. Now I see grass and trees below me. There's the tarmac. Helicopters and airplanes sitting on the tarmac. Soon I'll be sailing over the runway.

Runway?

"Oh, right," I thought. "This is a military base" These aircraft are off limits. What am I doing here? I need to go back. How do I get back? Close my eyes? No, open eyes. Look at hands. Look at my hands.

My eyes opened to the jarring scene of both my hands locked tightly on Dr. Bob Vereen's throat. His face was blue. His body hung heavy in my hands. In the muscle contractions and paralysis of electrocution by the Taser, I had involuntarily choked him to death.

It took an effort to open my fingers and let the body drop to the floor. I stood there, not knowing what to do.

"Lieutenant Dassett!" came a familiar whisper.

"Pratt!"

"Lieutenant! I got my discharge! You need a ride out of here?"

Pratt drove off the base through the front gate with me hiding in the trunk.

Is This Vision Inevitable?

Locked condos stretch for miles across the land,
With windows fortified by bars of steel
And indoor malls, enclosed arenas, and
Hospitals where the privileged may heal
Or die and exit through an airlock seal.
Outside, polluted air and climate change
Harm those who can't afford the condo deal.

Time Adjusters

Introduction

It is probable that more people have read about and/or discussed the Gysin/Burroughs technique of cutting up pages of text and rearranging them randomly to create spontaneous new passages, than have actually read a cut up book from cover to cover. There is a reason for that.

Burroughs himself, in a 1966 letter to Gysin, said, "Many fans told me they found the Olympia edition (of *The Soft Machine*) difficult to read . . . Reading the book over I could see the point . . . there was not enough narrative material to carry such a load of cut ups and unrelated descriptive passages. So I attempted to give the book a narrative structure."[1]

Burroughs called the cut up method a "sifting panning process,"[2] and allowed that initial juxtaposition of words "must be edited and rearranged as in any other method of composition."[3]

By 1968, Burroughs may have found the best use for cut ups. In a letter to Carl Weissner, he announced that he was "going back to straight narrative," but would still use cut ups "as an integral part of narrative in delirium and flashback scenes."[4]

---

[1]*Rub Out the Words The Letters of William S. Burroughs 1959-1974*, ed. Bill Morgan (New York: Harper Collins, 2012), p. 243

[2]*Ibid.*, p. 44

[3]*Ibid.,* p. 105

[4]*Ibid.*, p. 276

It is in this spirit that my science fiction story, *Time Adjusters*, contains brief interludes of cut-up and stream-of-consciousness material to approximate the fragmentation of time and space in an otherwise (more or less) straight narrative.

Bill Ectric, Saint Augustine, Florida, 2012

Time Adjusters

∞

The 1980s were a strange time for me. As much as I wanted to accept the amenities and corporate trappings, I couldn't shake the feeling that something was wrong.

Exhausted from working all day in an open bay warehouse under the hot Florida sun, I applied for an entry-level job in the mailroom of the prestigious American Wage Insurance Company. They hired me. My first day of work in the 36-story building was like entering an air-conditioned promised land.

Here is something I scribbled on a yellow post-it pad during fifteen-minute morning break:

The wheels are turning now. Wires crackle. Fields in harvest. People water plants for us in the sunny atrium. Every American can read about good health and opportunity in the grocery store checkout line. Light refreshments. I want to play my Donald Fagan album on the intercom to all 36 floors. I want coffee to taste as good as it smells. Endless paper clips - why would they ever need to manufacture another paper clip?

∞

The robed priest lowered his knife blade toward Lisa's chest. Her cute, naked body lay helplessly on a stone slab. The soft spread of her buttocks emphasized the hardness of the stone, and when she raised her head, I could see the where the slab had pressed her 1980s lacquered hair flat in back.

Ape-like creatures stood, two on each side, holding her arms and legs.

The simian guards repeated the chant of the priest.

"Ahh, Flahhh, Ahhh, Gamo!"

"Ahhhh, Flahhhhh, Ahhhhh Gamohhhh!"

Their chant seemed to open unfamiliar avenues in my own brain, giving rise to a violent goal. Kill the phony priest.

Kids playing, running, hiding, laughing.
"Haste!" shouted Jeff. "Haste to this silly contraption of flight!"
Somebody's older brother tossing baseball cards into the air.
"Up for grabs!" he yelled as the cards came fluttering down. This was his way of leaving his childhood behind. I got both Mickey Mantle and Roger Maris. But where are they now? Recklessness! Sometimes I find them, old and faded; other times they are brand new and slick. You can still smell the bubble gum. But sometimes I open the top drawer of my dresser and they are not there at all.

∞

In 1986, I paid a thousand dollars cash for a white 1980 Toyota Celica Hatchback. The guy who placed the ad in the Auto Trader magazine said it was in perfect running condition and he wanted twelve hundred, but I talked him down by suggesting I might have a mechanic look at it first. He said forget the mechanic, one thousand, as is.

The car felt solid, well built. It was fast and handled great going through the gears. It looked rugged and sleek simultaneously.

I say I bought the Toyota in 1986, but there are times when I remember going somewhere, like a concert or a party that I *know* happened in '82 or '83, yet I remember going in that car. The memory of persistence? Automatic image annotation and retrieval?

Lisa and I were traveling up the coast on old Florida Highway A1A when my Celica broke down in the middle of nowhere. The engine light dimmed as we coasted to a stop on the side of the road. I stepped out of the car. The silence of the deserted highway filled me with the sensation that time was standing still. An orange sunset made silhouettes of the shrubs and low-lying palm fronds on the left side of the road, beyond which lay undeveloped swampland. Time wafted back into motion once again when, from the other side of the road, a gentle easterly breeze carried the salty smell of the ocean over dunes and scrub brush. Dark evening wings overhead.

I opened the hood. Battery cables seemed tight enough. The fan belt felt snug when I tugged on it.

I slid back into the driver's seat and said, "We passed a little bar less than a mile back. We could walk back there and use the phone, or maybe get somebody to tow us to the nearest mechanic."

Lisa shoved a folder under her seat and rifled through her wallet for a Triple-A card.

"Don't ask anyone to tow you," she said. "They'll be drunk. Just call Triple-A to come and tow the car. I'll stay here."

"Out here by yourself? I don't want to leave you alone out here."

"I'll lock the doors. I don't want to carry the folder to a bar, and I don't want to leave it here unguarded. And I'm wearing heels."

She wasn't actually wearing them. Lisa had kicked off her shoes some time ago for comfort, but I knew what she meant.

"I still don't like leaving you here," I said.

"I'm telling you, I'll be alright. I'll lock the doors. Here, take the Triple-A. Just try not to take too long, and get back to me as soon as possible, okay?"

"Okay."

"I don't want to be here all night."

"Let's make sure all the doors are locked. I'll walk fast. Button up your blouse."

"Don't ask anyone for help, just call Triple-A, and hurry back."

I got out of the car, closed the hood, and watched Lisa reach over and push the lock button on the driver's side. I tried to open it, just to be sure, but it was secure. Then I walked around to the passenger side and made sure she had locked that door as well.

I heard the sound of distant ocean waves as I walked back in the direction from whence we came.

Two Harley-Davidson motorcycles were parked in front of Bob's Bait Shop and Bar, a ramshackle structure divided into two parts, each with its own separate entrance. The bait shop was closed, but a neon Budweiser sign glowed in the window of the bar.

When my eyes adjusted to the bar's dark interior, I saw two bikers playing pool under one of those Budweiser carousels in which a team of Clydesdale horses pulled a beer wagon around in circles through the snow. There must have been an electrical problem with the carousel, because the light sometimes flickered inside it and the horses lurched forward, but then the light went dim, and those hawses weren't going anywhere.

That's just like me, I thought. I can sit here and go nowhere, or I can walk and walk, or drive for miles, but some kind of loop keeps bringing me back to nowhere.

The place was almost empty, except for the bartender, the two bikers, an old man sitting at the end of the bar, a large parrot perched on a stand, and me. Lights blinked on an old jukebox that played a country song I didn't recognize.

I walked around the pool tables to the bar, which covered the entire length of the back wall.

"Do you have a phone I can use?"

"Only for paying customers," drawled the bartender.

"Bud in the bottle," I said. "My car broke down…"

I started to tell him that Lisa was waiting for me, but somehow, that sounded lame, leaving my girlfriend stranded and alone.

"My brother-in-law runs a towing service," said the bar man, "I'll give him a call him. Take him a while to get here, but hey, you ain't drivin' so you free to drink a few, huh?"

He turned and disappeared into a back room through a curtain of beads.

I sat down on a barstool. One of the barstool legs was a quarter-inch too short, allowing me to rock absent-mindedly to the steady, mid-tempo beat of the music.

The beer was ice cold and delicious. My mind drifted back to the day I first got involved in the time-light-bending problem at the American Wage Insurance Company. I felt awkward at first, wearing a dress-shirt, a tie, slacks, and loafers. The preppies and yuppies of my own age or younger seemed to be in on some knowledge to which I was a stranger. Like I wasn't sophisticated, and I was older than some of them. Nevertheless, I enjoyed seeing the girls in their hose and expensive skirts and high heels, hairstyles and perfume.

A couple of the girls seemed to like talking to me. One of them was Lisa. She had started out in the Mail Room just like me but was now an Assistant Underwriter. Her real interest was fraud investigation and she had taken some chemistry and forensics classes at night. By '80s standards, her sandy blonde hairstyle was only moderately big and sculpted with Aqua Net.

Lisa and I met because of Arthur "Arth" Hampton III, the 23 year-old surfer grandson of the president of the company. Arth was the coolest person I met at American Wage, besides Lisa. Even though he came from wealth, he was casual and unassuming. I felt comfortable around him. He readily admitted that he would rather surf than work in an office. He listened to rock music. He and I could talk about which bars at the beach were the best. We both liked Frank Zappa.

"Check out Zappa's Baby Snakes video," he told me. "With Terry Bozzio on drums."

"That's the one with clay animation by Bruce Bickford, right?"

"Yeah, and it's got footage from a 1977 Halloween concert and all kinds of shit."

"I've seen clips of that animation on TV!"

I learned gradually that Arth tended to hide a keen, intuitive intelligence behind a beach-bum, slacker image. Well, he really was kind of a slacker, too. I didn't blame him for not wanting to do the dreary day-to-day paperwork. I wouldn't have done it, either, if I didn't have to. One time Lisa expressed surprise when Arth explained how the Italian violinist, Paganini, had been the inspiration for a guitar composition by Steve Via, which was featured in the movie *Crossroads*.

Arth, who had a way of saying things with wry humor in his voice, told her, "I'm a dichotomy..."

There were always magazines lying around in the break room. I took a page from *Newsweek* and a page from *Entertainment Magazine*, cut them up with scissors, and mixed them together. This was an idea I got from reading about an artist named Brion Gysin and a writer named William Burroughs.

Continuing our retrospective of this decade's movie blockbusters, Reagan appeared on national television to say the weapons transfers had an Australian post-apocalyptic Mad Max 2. Volumes of documents relating to the scandal were destroyed by renegade androids and the subject of an arms embargo aimed at younger audiences.

Operation Iranian Crossroads, a diplomatic blues mission. Old Scratch, kid.

Between free minutes, a legendary American headed victim. One Robert Johnson.

Arth told Lisa and me that his father, Arthur Hampton II, had refused to hire him.

"You don't have the maturity to take this work seriously," his dad had told him. "You haven't convinced me otherwise."

So, a few weeks ago, while his father was away in Japan on business, Arth had asked his grandfather for a job. The old man relented, having a soft spot in his heart for his carefree grandson.

"I can't wait to see Dad's face next month when he gets back from Japan," Arth told us.

Even though he had to wear a suit to work every day, Arth's approach was typically unencumbered. Having received a company expense account, he went to the clothier for a fitting. After they took his measurements, Arth ordered six identical blue-gray suits. One for each weekday plus one spare.

"That way," he said, "I don't have to think about it. All the suits hang side-by-side in my closet. When I'm down to two suits, I drop the other four off at the drycleaner."

Whenever he came to work in a slightly rumpled suit, we knew he he'd been too distracted by surfing, women, and beer to pick up his laundry at the cleaners.

Arth asked Lisa if she wanted to be on a committee to plan new procedures for the Underwriting Department. They needed two people, so she recommended me.

"What would I be doing?" I asked.

"Underwriters review applications for homeowners insurance and decided which property was acceptable to insure."

"I heard that Pete Dooley was interested in that."

"Arth said he would let me choose my partner," said Lisa. "He wants people who feel comfortable working together. He said experience isn't important because there are some new procedures that nobody has ever used before. Starting fresh."

Rumors of a new, controversial technology had everyone talking, but at this point, no one knew how accurate it was, or if it was even true.

The new technology used orbiting satellites to intercept light waves that bounced off the Earth's surface, bend these waves backwards through a series of prism & mirror relays, and back to Earth, thereby capturing future reflections of the Earth's topography, to analyze potential sites of floods, earthquakes, and other disasters. Nobody imagined that the enormous flux of energy between the Earth and the Sun would cause actual disruptions in time and space, but that is what happened.

The cost of homeowner's insurance often combines space and time into a single construct. An indivisible premium, ameliorated, tied to inflation, meaning that a single universe has three dimensions of space and one dimension of time. The dwelling policy (DP) is used for two aspects of a unified field theory. Special relativity homeowner's liability is adjusted to an inflation factor or a cost index. Scientific people know that Time is only a kind of seasonal/secondary residence, or age.

∞

Nighttime, in my apartment, I'm watching a 1960s TV show called *Death Valley Days*, starring Ronald Reagan as a cowboy. Reagan also did some of the commercials, still dressed as a cowboy, but stepping out of character to tell us that he and the rest of the crew use Borax waterless soap. Tonight, I notice he's holding something he calls antibacterial soap. It doesn't seem right. I call Lisa for the first time, having just asked her for her phone number in case we needed to discuss our underwriting project.

"Hello?"

"Lisa, this is Bill, from work."

"Oh, hi, Bill."

"Well, I see you gave me the right number."

"You're testing the number?" she sounded amused.

"No, I'm just kidding. I wanted to ask you something. It's kind of off-the-wall but you've studied chemistry, right?"

"I have."

"By any chance, do you know when antibacterial soap came out?"

"Came out? You mean, like, in stores?"

"Yeah, in stores."

"Pretty recently," she said. "I'm almost certain it was only within the last couple of years. Pete Dooley probably knows. You should ask him tomorrow."

"Good point. But it hasn't been around long, right? Definitely not as far back as the sixties."

"No. I mean, it might have been invented, but you didn't see it all over the place."

"Right," I said. "But I just saw a 1960s TV commercial with Ronald Reagan advertising antibacterial soap"

I filled her in about *Death Valley Days*.

"Maybe it was CGI," ventured Lisa.

"CGI?"

"Computer Generated Images, like in *Tron*."

"This looked like the real thing," I said.

"Well, they don't do the whole scene with the computer. They just insert a small object into an existing scene. They dub in new words. It's really cool what they can do!"

"I don't know," I said. "Maybe."

"What other explanation could there be? I don't think he would do a commercial as Governor."

"It couldn't have been when he was governor, anyway."

"What?"

"Still not recent enough."

"He's still governor, I'm pretty sure."

"You are joking, right?

"About what?"

That wasn't the first time I noticed things were getting strange.

∞

The square headlights of my white 1980 Toyota Celica flashed to high beam as I tried to get a better look at the two signs in front of a swampy tract of recently cleared land.

Lisa read the signs aloud, "Mangrove Construction, Future site of Moore Executive Center."

We sailed North along this desolate stretch of State Road A1A, past smatterings of scrub pines on sandy ridges, interspersed with more clearings in various states of development. Some tracts already bore concrete slabs or earth moving equipment.

Lisa said, "While you were sleeping late from watching reruns of *Death Valley Days* all night…"

"Research," I said. "Burning the midnight oil."

"Yes, well, while you were sleeping off your research, the FBI questioned me about the light-bending project," she said. "They want to talk to you next."

"How did it go?"

"Arth gave me a ride to the FBI building."

"You rode in his black Lamborghini?"

"Yeah, Arth said he wanted to be present when they interrogated his team members, but when we got there, they separated us."

"Did you have attorney present?"

"No, I supposedly have immunity."

"Supposedly?!"

"I don't know how these things work!"

"Well, Arth should know! Did they question him?"

"They've already questioned him a couple of times."

"What did they ask you?"

"Mostly stuff I really didn't know the answers to, about kilowatts and radiation levels. I told them the only thing I knew for sure was that after I got assigned to the project, everything came to a halt until further notice. But you'll never guess what I got."

"What?"

"A confidential file."

"From American Wage?"

"No, FBI."

"FBI? How the hell did you get that?"

"This is the funny part," said Lisa. "Arth told me later that he wasn't surprised when they separated us. But while he was waiting for me, he says, he acted so annoyed, that just to keep him occupied, an FBI supervisor invited him into his office to look at some new golf clubs. Next thing you know, Arth was inviting the supervisor and another agent to the golf course at TPC Sawgrass, and describing the course to them."

"Arth has a membership at Sawgrass?"

"His father does, but listen to my story. Arth told me the agents were cocky because most everyone they haul in gets nervous and submissive, except for Arth, who is never intimidated by anything, and I think he kind of out-alpha'd all the other males."

"Out alpha . . . ?"

"You know. He told me he's been around when his father and grandfather were dealing with bigwigs, and being comfortable helps the other person to be comfortable, and they let down their guard. While they're talking about golf, the supervisor gets called away for something. The other agent volunteers to make a coffee run and Arth tells the guy he wants Half & Half, two sugars, and an extra black coffee on the side, or some damn thing like that, so the agent goes for coffee. I'm walking down the hall toward the exit after being interrogated and Arth sticks his head out of a doorway and says, 'Psst! Lisa, here, take this,' and hands me a file, and says, 'There's a copier at the end of the hall...'"

"Why you?" I asked.

"Why me? I'm on his team! Besides, he couldn't do it; when the agent got back with the coffee they were going out on the veranda to smoke cigars!"

"How did you get the file back into the office?"

"Arth told me to leave it behind the copier and he would somehow get it back to where he found it."

"And you did it?"

"Yeah."

"And did he put it back?"

"I don't know, I forgot to ask. He must have."

"Where are the copies?"

Lisa reached under the passenger seat and pulled out the folder that contain pages from an FBI file she had photocopied without permission, when nobody was looking.

"Can we turn on the inside light?" she asked.

"Sure." I reached up and clicked on the overhead interior light. "What does it say?"

Lisa read from the file

Operation Caveman

Synopsis

The primitive anthropoids observed working at private loading docks are most closely related to Australopithecus Afarensis, which made its appearance in the evolutionary chain approximately three million years ago. The main differences are, while Australopithecus (hereafter referred to as Austra for singular, Austras for plural) rarely grew taller than five feet, these anthropoids are approximately six feet in height, with massively developed upper bodies and vice-like strength in their hands, making them well-suited to the heavy physical labor they were performing. The females have noticeably larger hips and breasts but seem to share equally in the work. Facial characteristics of these Austras are more simian than human, with low foreheads ridged prominently over the eyes, flat noses, and protruding jaws with sharp teeth. They wear steel-toed boots and overalls, but we assume that their bodies are as hairy as their exposed arms, hands, shoulders, and heads. The anthropoids apparently work at the loading dock by choice, not under compulsion, most likely in return for compensation. Whether this compensation is in the form of money or some other rewarded we have yet to determine The Austras do not appear to have any political agenda or affiliation and, nor is there any evidence that they are aligned with a union.

Before I could comment on the FBI report, the *check engine* light came and I felt the car slowing down, even as I pressed on the gas pedal.

"Damn!"

"What is it?" said Lisa. "What's wrong?"

"Engine trouble."

"Déjà vu, too."

"I was thinking the same thing."

"Déjà vu, too."

"I was think… hey!"

∞

Developed by a company called Global Interlinear, the Light Bending Technology had both champions and opponents, usually divided along the lines of conservative and liberal politics. The liberal vice-presidential candidate had written a book about saving Mother Earth in which he said, "The current use of Light Bending Future Form Capture is placing an unfair disadvantage on the poor by targeting future disaster areas and denying coverage. Then there are the unknown effects on the environment and the actual bending of time itself." The conservatives called that the crackpot theory and said, no, it is not really reflections of the future, but simply predictors, like seismographs for earthquakes and volcanoes. The public drove to work each day listening to these debates on the radio as if it didn't mean a hill of beans.

Look for the LABEL: The Beastie Boys' Fifth Rose, 11 per cent by volume in real terms. Cautious correspondence and diversification of hip-hop genre into more complex style of old-fashioned Keynesian stimulus. Sample it, Brother Volcker. Double-digit Loop!

NOTIFICATION TO RECIPIENTS: If you have the power of media context, which gave many of these passing phenomena greater innovation, the crisis of malaise, the Adventures of Grandmaster Flash, and self-confidence, it's Morning in America, popping out of black backgrounds, a startling contrast to jelly beans.

The Underwriting Department was on the 19th floor. It was a lengthy office space with plush carpet and a row of ten cubicles placed considerately along the large plate glass windows, so of shops, restaurants, bars, and other attractions looked deceptively small from the 19th floor. Within the semicircle was an outdoor courtyard where people strolled around, sat on benches, watched a clown make balloon animals, and threw coins into the decorative fountain. The open side of the semicircle faced the Saint Johns River. Boats and yachts could dock there come for special events. Further out, the occasional sailboat or barge drifted by. The scene was beautiful on a nice day, and thrilling on a dark, stormy day.

But back to the office. Across the aisle from our row of cubicles, against the inside wall, stood a copying machine, fax machine, microfiche, and a table with various forms arranged on it. At one end of the department was a break room with tables and chairs, coffee maker, snack machine, refrigerator, and sink. At the other end of the oblong room was the office of Mr. Thompson, or as we called him, The Bear. A big, jovial middle-aged man, Mr. Thompson was

Department Head of Underwriting, as well as one of the Vice-Presidents of American Wage Insurance Company.

Arth, with an unlit cigarette perched casually over his ear, asked Lisa and I to join him in The Bear's den, which is what he called Mr. Thompson's office. Arth's grandfather, Company President Arthur Hampton, Sr., was in there, as well. They had already been discussing the New Project and wanted to meet Lisa and me.

Mr. Hampton's manner put us at ease. Sparkling eyes under bushy eyebrows softened his creased face. He spoke to Lisa and me in a low voice, as though taking us into his confidence.

"I just wanted to meet you," said Mr. Hampton. "Mr. Thompson tells me that you are both bright, eager to learn, and that I can count on you to be professional. Arth says you like video games and are comfortable with computers and other cutting-edge technology, like satellite communication. AND, I'm also counting on you to keep an eye on this grandson of mine, and to keep HIM professional, will you?"

"Granddad," Arth smiled as he popped the unlit cigarette in his mouth, "You know us business executives need to stop and smell the roses once in a while."

"Yeah," said Mr. Hampton, still looking at Lisa and me. He motioned his thumb toward Arth and said, "This one likes to stop and smell the sea oats!"

This was a reference to the tall coastal grass lining the inland edges of the beach. The old man knew Arth liked to surf during working hours.

We weren't told any specifics about the New Project during that meeting.

Mr. Thompson walked us out of his office, saying, "I'm sure you have some work to finish up before we get underway."

"I'm going down to the newsstand," said Arth.

Mr. Thompson gave a hearty laugh and said, "You never read a newspaper in your life!"

Arth smiled good-naturedly and said, with the cigarette still dangling from his lips, "Did I say anything about reading a newspaper?"

This was apparently an ongoing joke between them. Since there was no smoking allowed in the building, Arth always said he was going down to the newsstand when he wanted a smoke. That's when I walked past Pete Dooley's cubicle, where he sat glaring at me bitterly. He became motionless, as if frozen in the act of wiping his computer terminal screen with a damp paper towel, frowning at me.

Dooley could have been anywhere between thirty and forty years old. He had a neatly barbered salt & pepper flattop haircut, a forehead stippled by some long-settled contest between worry lines and acne, shoulders hunched like a repressed vulture, and slimness due more to poor nutrition than fitness. His clip-on bowties, well-pressed white dress shirts and black slacks were at odds with the clodhopper work shoes he wore every day, reminding me of a preacher in one of the more austere Protestant denominations.

Liquid screen cleaner ran down the terminal screen from the wet paper towel he still held pressed against the screen in mid-swab. Dooley turned quickly away from me and continued cleaning. I noticed how organized and immaculate he kept his cubicle. No paper clips, rubber bands, unfiled folders, or personal items cluttered his desk, not even a photograph. He spaced his telephone, stapler, and desk calendar in a straight line, an equal distance from each other. At the far end of Dooley's desk were a spray can of Lysol, a spray bottle of screen cleaner, and a pump dispenser bottle of hand sanitizer.

I started mixing insurance forms into my cut-ups, just for fun. The American Wage Insurance Company had grown so big that they now printed all their own application forms, policies, policy riders, stationary, and other documents. The print shop was actually below ground, under the first floor lobby, the basement. When forms got crumpled up in the printer, or when the ink wasn't dark enough, they were shredded, so it's not like I was stealing forms.

Claimant: Downey
Profile: Buck Adolescent. Notably engaged. future Suburbs.
Cause of damage: Jock nerd oversight
Losses: Club, records, uncle

Adjuster: Schumacher
Profile: Early sort. Uses diamond covered, pack-trained collaborative actors.
Damage Assessment: Deal with the Devil
Payout: Below Zero

Claimant: Sheedy
Profile: Twenties. Witness of the Dean. Caribbean.
Cause of damage: Ideological member
Loss: Ceremonial Hall, television, pretty old scratch

Adjuster: Estevez
Profile: Possessed floater. Commonly implies unknown tribe. Class rider.
Damage Assessment: 16 candles, arson
Payout: Breakfast and play money

∞

"Pascua Florida!" shouted the Spanish conquistador.

That is Spanish for "Flowery Festival" or "Flowery Easter," which is what Ponce de Leon said when he and his crew arrived by ship in Saint Augustine, Florida, only days ago. Another ship had found its way from Atlantic Ocean to the Saint Johns River, via the Intercostal Waterway, and docked near the Riverfront Mall. The Mall is a kind of mall or plaza with a courtyard and fountains and lot of stores and restaurants, but only a part of the building was visible. The jungle explorers were gathered around a fire in jungle-like

105

woods, yet only a few yards away was a section of the popular clothing store, Banana Republic, as though it had appeared from another time.

A Spanish Conquistador exclaimed, "Cantando árboles!" which I later found out meant "Singing trees." He referred to the music emanating from audio speakers hidden in the landscaped plants, flowers and freshly sculpted crepe myrtle trees.

I watched from the second floor of the warped-off structure, above the Banana Republic, near the entrance of Fat Tuesday's, a bar with a Mardi Gras motif that served those icy slush drinks, potent with alcohol. The Spanish explorers began, warily at first, to approach the 1980s shoppers, who may or may not have assumed that the Spaniards were dressed for some Mall publicity event, the way the employees at Banana Republic always dressed in safari gear. I caught sight of Arth Hampton carrying a tray of drinks into the midst of the foreign explorers. Laughter and revelry echoed against the walls. The Banana Republic's tight-jeaned safari girls and Fat Tuesday's Mardi Gras gaudy green, purple and gold excess seemed perfectly in step with the 16th Century uniforms of the Spanish Conquistadors.

∞

The jukebox in the small dark bar played the same song again. Not quite country and not quite rock, neither fast or slow, but satisfying with its spring-loaded rhythm and reliable beat. A biker built like a bull was racking billiard balls for another game of pool. He was bald with a think roll of flesh on the back his neck. His long sideburns curved up and joined under his nose to form a mustache, but no beard. After placing the last ball in the rack, he slid the wooden triangle into position, bracing the balls with his fingertips so they would slide, not roll, on the felt table surface, and deftly removed the rack, leaving a perfect triangle of balls. The other biker approached, pool cue in hand, stroking his long gray beard. His silver earring reflected red and blue light from the flickering Budweiser carousel above the pool table.

A bird, perched on a stand near the pool table, squawked, "Awwwk! Floreeda!" This caused one of the man with the grat beard to hesitate in making his pool shot. He looked at the bird and then resumed the game. Just as he lined up his stick, the bird squawked again.

"SQUAWWWK! Paska Floreeda!"

The man gripped his pool stick like a baseball bat and swung it, *whacking* the bird's head clean off. The head went flying and landed with a plop into a full glass of whiskey where an old man sat nodding at the end of the bar. The splash woke the man up. It was hard to tell if he was weeping or laughing as he wheezed a heartfelt response to the grisly surprise in his drink.

I said, "You killed the crow!"

"It's not a crow," said the tall, bearded dude who had whacked the bird's head. "Why did you say crow?"

So now I'm being questioned about the bird.

The bartender said, "I'm gonna try to call my brother-in-law again," having never mentioned that the first call was unsuccessful. He disappeared once more into the back room.

The old man was snoring.

The other biker, with the sideburns mustache, walked around the table and joined the one holding the stick. They both looked at me seriously.

"What?" I asked.

"Why did you call it a crow?"

"I don't know, I..."

"Do you work with crows?" asked graybeard, frowning at me.

I said, "I work for American Wage Insurance."

They looked at each other in surprise.

I said, "Maybe I got that TV commercial on my mind."

I remembered one of the ad slogans for our company; a TV commercial. It shows an airplane delivering supplies to hurricane victims. As the plane takes off, the camera pans over to a crow up on top of a wet tree, and a voice says, "American Wage delivers the help you need. Faster. As the crow flies." They also have a big poster like this at the airport.

"You know," I tried to shrug it off. "As the crow flies?"

"What's that supposed to mean?"

"It's just a slogan," I said. "For American Wage Insurance Company."

"What do you do for American Wage?"

"I'm in the Underwriting Department."

The two bikers looked at each other.

"Underwriting," said mustache to graybeard.

"You probably know Arth Hampton," said Mustache Man.

"So?" I asked. "Mr. Hampton owns the entire company, if that's what you mean."

"I bet you guys have had to answer a lot of questions lately," said the bald biker.

"Did you happen to pick up anything while answering questions," asked the other biker, stroking his gray beard.

"What do you mean?" I asked.

"You come in here gabbin' about crows."

"I came in here gabbin' about nothing."

"You went picking up things that don't belong to you? Reading about prehistoric times?" asked Fat-Necked Baldy.

I couldn't think of anything to say. My mouth was dry from apprehension. I took a big swig of beer.

"Did you remove a file from someplace?" the gray-bearded Harley rider finally came out with it. "Maybe around the time you were being questioned? Just tell us the truth and you won't be in any trouble. We just need to know."

Graybeard opened his chained leather wallet and showed me a badge.

"FBI," he said. "I'm Leonard, this is Skinnerd, or as I like to call him, skin-head. Maybe you can help us."

"Are those your real names?"

"Did you steal an FBI files?"

"No. Why? What are you talking about?"

"But you know who did."

"Why would I know anything about a… a, what did you call it?"

"You're an underwriter, aren't you?"

"Learning to be," I said.

"Well, the file went missing after we interrogated everybody in the Underwriting Department."

Changing the subject, I asked, "What's all this about crows?"

"Well," said Leonard, still holding the pool cue, "I've only had to capture or kill about a hundred crows which all had satellite chips implanted in them."

"But," I said hesitantly. "That wasn't a crow you just killed. You said so yourself."

"Yeah," he mused. "I guess I've just reached the point where I hate all birds."

I suddenly remembered Lisa.

"Can you give me and my girlfriend a ride to Kingsland, Georgia?"

"Is she the girl in the white Toyota Celica?" asked Leonard.

"Yeah, how did you…"

"One of our guys towed your car and gave her a ride back to Jacksonville. Made sure she got home safe."

"But we were headed to Kingsland," I protested.

"You don't want to go to Kingsland," said Skinnerd. "We'll give you a ride back to Jacksonville. And, seeing as you've been reading our files, which by the way, is a crime, we might as well tell you what's going on. We're willing to overlook the theft if you help us. It's hard enough to tell who's on who's side, or if there is even a side to be on. Your company agreed to deactivate the big dish in Key West, but somebody's been putting small chips on crows, so when an entire flock flies from point A to point B, they act as one big satellite dish to catch the light waves. It only takes a couple of minutes to get a reading, and the deed is done."

"But every time they do it," continued Leonard, "Something happens somewhere. Different times merge in certain locations. We've been following this shit for weeks. We've lost people! They disappear!"

"What about the cavemen?" I asked.

"The *Austras,*" said Skinnerd. "Australopithecus. And the Spanish explorers, and God knows what else. We're trying to keep tabs on them. Hell, the CIA is trying to keep tabs on them. But it's become a political issue, and a Constitutional issue, with some people calling for us to leave them alone, other people saying to send them back, and besides, there are more urgent matters to attend to."

"Like what, exactly?"

"The whole insurance thing!" said Leonard. "You must have heard about it on the news. Nobody who needs insurance ever seems to have it. Epidemic of bad timing they call it at the newsstand. It's always the same. They think their home is covered, but as soon as they have a claim and the adjuster goes out to examine the damage, it turns out the policy has lapsed. Some call it an 'epidemic of bad timing' while others suspect the adjusters are pirating Time-Light technology and triggering retro-non-renewals when they detect a future loss."

"What do you want me to do?"

"We want you to go back to work and gather information for us, but it's gonna be weird."

"It's already weird," I said. "Who's the President?"

They looked at each other.

"Chester A. Arthur," said Skinnerd.

"Oh, God!" I wailed, feeling dizzy.

"Just kidding!" snorted Skinnerd. "It's Reagan."

"Asshole!"

"Sorry, man."

"Which term?"

"It varies."

I had no intention of spying on my friends at American Wage, but I went along with Leonard and Skinnerd just to buy some time, talk to Lisa and Arth, and figure out what to do next. The FBI agents gave me a ride to what used to be the Riverfront Mall, the big plaza full of shops and restaurants. But there were trees all around. We were in the jungle-like woods that existed here in the 1500's. Just a section of the Mall was here, like it was chopped off and set down in the forest: The Banana Republic clothing store was on the first floor. On top of that was Fat Tuesday's, the wild purple & green bar, a flight of metal steps leading up to the bar's second-floor entrance. At the bottom of those steps was the courtyard fountain surrounded by trees that extended into the Spanish explorer's campsite. Not far from here was the American Wage Insurance building.

While people must have been aware of this bizarre situation, they were somehow adjusting as if they were either in denial, or maybe they perceived the changes as gradual, the way parts of a city can change over time so you don't notice it.

At least we didn't have to worry about Pete Dooley every day. He had requested, and received, a transfer to the company Print Shop, where he could do an "honest days work and avoid the office politics," as he liked to say.

∞

The 1980s were not completely void of guideposts. Max Headroom tried to tell me about William Gibson and cyberspace, nattering from the television screen in my apartment, but even as he mouthed the words, I heard something different. Comic books wanted to jump from the newsstand into my hands, but I thought, incorrectly, "too grown up watch the Watchmen." Philip K. Dick's aura still lingered strongly, reminding me to keep my watch and check in on a regular basis. This I accomplished by cutting up and rearranging pages from magazines, books about art and printing, movies, and world events.

The key to light drove parliament sideways over rolling magpies. Rollicking industrialists frolic in new club polo shirts. Oh, grievous chimp. Aluminum blue soul congregates inside limits of peace.

Where do years even begin with "lithos" from Warhol to Abraham, Dali to Delacroix?

Goya would spare the last old limestone lithograph of Abraham. Water is faith, right. The Sacrificial poster is different after drawing with a crayon-brushed hand. Rather not a description, more a symbol, chemical kill, must place Kierkegaard third, lamb takes his question instead. Foxe's Book of Martyrs. Killed on the retelling. Limestone acts with Warhol during Isaac's other medium, though for Cappiello to begin, his father allows the Beatles on question his world.

∞

Pete Dooley confronted Lisa one day in the break room when he thought they were alone.

She and I were on our afternoon break, around 2:45 PM, the only ones in the break room. Lisa sat down at one of the tables as I walked over to the coffee maker.

"Just enough left for two cups," I said. "The good stuff."

"Hmmm, the strong, bitter stuff," she said.

"Want me to make more?"

"No, it'll be okay." She picked up a handful of sugar packets from a bowl on the table and leaned forward, looking into the bowl, saying, "I don't see any Sweet'n Low in here."

"I'll get some from the pantry," I said, placing the two cups of coffee on the table.

Inside the small, walk-in supply closet known as the pantry, I scanned the shelves. Cups, napkins, dairy creamer, Little Debbie Snack Cakes, and, aha, there it was, a big box full of little packets of Sweet'n Low.

Just then, a familiar voice jarred my nerves with its cracked, high pitch.

"I know what you're doing!"

It was Pete Dooley talking to Lisa. I could see her sitting at the table, looking up at him. The half-open pantry door blocked my view of Dooley and blocked his view of me.

"What?" said Lisa.

"I know what you're up to," said Dooley, somewhat nervously. "I don't have to put up with it."

"What are you talking about?" she said, a bit nervous herself.

"Using your influence," said Dooley. "Using it to get what you want and skip right over people. Because it's not about who does the best job anymore. I could file a grievance, but I know they would take your side."

Lisa looked worriedly at me for help. Dooley followed her gaze as I walked out of the pantry. I thought I heard him gasp quietly when he saw me, but he quickly recovered his composure.

"I don't care who hears me!" he said. Then, to Lisa, he added, "Are you aware you are destroying the ozone with that hairspray?"

I had to stifle a laugh as Dooley turned and marched out the door.

"What was that all about?" I asked.

"I think he applied for your job and didn't get it, because Arth asked for my input and I chose you."

"Has he been with the company a long time?"

Before Lisa could answer my question, young surfer Arth walked casually into the break room wearing a slightly rumpled blue-gray suit.

"What crawled up Dooley's ass?" he asked.

"He was really rude to Lisa, man," I said. "What's that guy's problem?"

"What'd he say?" asked Arth. "Hey, if I make some more coffee will you help me drink it?"

"He was talking about filing a grievance or something," said Lisa. "I can't drink any more coffee. I don't even want the one I've got."

"Oh? Are you sure?"

"It's old."

"Can't be too old," said Arth. "Unless they made it yesterday."

"It's fine," I said. "What's Dooley's problem?"

"How long has Dooley worked for American Wage?" asked Lisa.

"Long time," said Arth, picking up Lisa's cup of coffee. "His mother worked here for, like, twenty years. Pete got hired just before she retired, then she died."

"Aww, that's sad," said Lisa.

Arth continued, "He's worked at entry level in almost every department. Doesn't get along with many people, but nobody wants to fire him."

"He's weird," I said.

Arth, in that way he had of saying things with wry humor in his voice, added, "He's a legacy."

∞

The Spanish Conquistadors made their way from Saint Augustine up to Jacksonville because they heard about the Mayport Naval Station. Then somebody told them about the Subs. Probably

Arth. Of courses, they had to see those! According to rumor, the Base Captain allowed one of the Conquistadors to board a submarine, which then submerged briefly for a routine drill, and the Spaniard disappeared. After a thorough search, someone theorized that he had returned to his own time, either because the time-light waves couldn't penetrate the combination of deep water and the hull of the sub, or because it was a nuclear powered submarine, or both. It was haphazard as hell, like most things the government wants us to believe they have under control.

Lisa and I were not as drastically removed from our own time as the Conquistadors or the *Austras*, but we wanted out of the disconcerting day-to-day fragmentation. We thought the base in Kingsland held the solution, if we could only get there.

Spare that resignation. Claims process has own ethic invented.

Where do years even begin with "lithos" from Warhol to Abraham to Delacroix?

Goya would spare 1798 a different faiths, last old limestone lithograph of Abraham, water is faith, right. The Sacrificial poster is different after drawing with a crayon-brushed hand. Rather not a description, more a symbol, chemical kill, must place Kierkegaard third, lamb takes his question instead. Foxe's Book of Martyrs Killed on the retelling. Limestone acts with Warhol during Isaac's other medium, though for Cappiello to begin, his father allows the Beatles on question his world.

∞

It was sort of business as usual in the American Wage Insurance building. People were trying to carry on their usual routine, like the British during the air raids in World War II. I reported to the Underwriting Department. We were told not to talk to the media about the Time/Light Bending debacle, which we officially would not use until further investigation.

115

Arth Hampton was teaching two Spanish explorers, Juan and Cristo, how to surf in return for one of their 16th Century metal helmets. This typically took place during Arth's extended lunch breaks.

Once, Lisa and I joined them on the beach during our lunch break. I parked my white Toyota Celica beside Arth's black Lamborghini. My tie fluttered in the wind as I walked around the car to open her door. Lisa slipped off her shoes and stockings and scrunched little bare footprints in the sand.

Out on the ocean, Cristo caught a wave. I watched him rise up on his long surfboard, plant his feet, and balance with his arms as a rolling wave lifted his him and his board up and forward, toward the shore. He wore neon-bright Hawaiian swimming trunks. He fell into the water and disappeared for a moment, then stood up in the shallow water and approached us, carrying his surfboard. Behind his wet black beard and mustache, he seemed to have a big smile on his face. His ears, nose, and forehead were tan, but his body was relatively pale from wearing a long-sleeved uniform and chainmail. Arth and Juan rode the next wave toward the shore in similar fashion.

At sunset, our group migrated to a popular nautical themed bar on the Beachfront Boardwalk called Seadog Willy's. The jukebox was playing the song *Brandy* by Looking Glass. Lisa and I were drinking Coronas and standing in front of the jukebox, which was, deciding what songs to play next. At a nearby table, Arth sat pouring shots of Tequila for Juan, Cristo, and himself, demonstrating the salt and lime custom. Arth was wearing the helmet. They had entered that alcohol-induced looseness that transcends language barriers, talking excitedly, grasping and repeating words and phrases from each other's language.

Cristo poked at his own chest, saying, "Corazón!"

"Heart?" said Arth. "Heart!"

"Corazón!"

"Corszawn!"

"Heart!" said Cristo.

Their table erupted with laughter.

A little while later I happened to see Arth in the men's room.

"That Cristo is a character!" said Arth. "You know what he said?"

"What?"

"He told me that when his ship was anchored off the coast Mexico, they saw an Aztec funeral for a Mexican elder who died of old age, and these Aztec's ate the dead man's heart."

"He saw it?"

"Yeah, but some of his fellow soldiers went back to Spain and told everybody the Aztecs were rampant cannibals, so they would have a better excuse to attack 'em and take over their country."

"Bastards!" I said.

"But that's not the best part. Somehow the word got back to the Aztecs about what he said, which of course pissed 'em off, so when these Spanish soldiers returned to Mexico, the Aztecs said, alright, fuckers, and ate the son-of-a-bitches for real!"

"No way!"

"Alive!"

Arth and I returned to the table laughing like it was the funniest thing we'd ever heard.

"What's so funny," asked Lisa.

Arth and I just laughed and shook our heads. Arch poured everyone another shout of Tequila and slapped Cristo on the back.

At two o'clock in the morning, Arth, Lisa, and I were sitting on barstools outside on the patio at Seadog Willie's, facing away from the bar, looking at all the empty tables and chairs. Arth was blowing smoke rings into the air. The Conquistadors had returned to their camp. The bar was closed, but Arth knew the owner, who said we could hang out while he was inside cashing out the registers. I leaned back and rested my arms on the bar, so that one of my arms was touching Lisa's back.

I was just about to close my arm around her when Lisa stood up and walked to a magazine rack against the far wall, next to the door.

It was a rack of free publications, like the Auto-Trader, the Beach-Trader, Entertainment Weekly, and so forth, but Lisa picked out one we had never seen before, called ***Veridical***. She opened the magazine and read aloud from it:

In 1981, embryonic stem cells taken from mouse embryos. Those who came before us theorized that John F. Kennedy was antichrist due to the passage in the Book of Revelation that says the "beast" will suffer a lethal wound to the head, but will then rise from the dead. Now, however, while Ronald Reagan cannot run for a third consecutive term, we must consider the possibility that he will return. If the prophet of Revelation interpreted Alzheimer's disease as a "head wound" and the new stem cell research will regenerate Reagan's brain, thus fulfilling the prophecy with space-age efficiency. Of course it would be done with space-age efficiency! Look at how the Food and Drug Administration, in 1972, demanded that contact lenses manufacturers use space-age plastic instead of glass. And what technology enabled this to be done with plastics that would not scratch the eyeball?

NASA!
NERO!
NOVUM!

Lisa interrupted her reading to interject, "Reagan has Alzheimer's? I haven't heard…"

"Let me see that?" said Arth.

Lisa handed the magazine to him.

"60 pound white offset paper stock," said Arth. "This is what we print our policies on."

Lisa asked, "Does Pete Dooley still work in the print shop?"

"Nobody works down there now," said Arth. "When the forest materialized outside the building it caused structural damage. The Saint Johns River is too close for comfort. One crack and the basement could flood."

"My God," I said. "Is it even safe to go into the building?"

"Yeah, the basement walls aren't load-bearing. There's a whole separate foundation, outside and separate from the basement walls. The Print Shop could flood and it would be like having a swimming pool in the basement, but the rest of the building would be fine. In theory."

"Then where has Dooley been?" I asked.

"Yeah," said Lisa. "Because this sound just like something he would write."

"You know why Dooley never got promoted?" Arth said.

"Because he's crazy?" I asked.

"That never stopped us before," said Arth. "No, he threatened one of our adjusters for denying a claim on some storefront church he was working with. The Old Man wanted to fire him on the spot."

"Why didn't he?"

"Hell, man . . . Granddad says it's harder to fire people than you think."

"It's got to be him," said Lisa. "Printing this…what's it called…Veridical? What does that even mean?"

"No idea," I said.

"Something about…something," said Arth. "The future, maybe?"

"What happened to the church?" I asked.

"Fire," said Arth. "Electrical, I think. But their policy had lapsed. There was nothing we could do for them."

"If Dooley threatened an adjuster," I said. "I don't understand why you guys didn't fire him."

"Well," said Arth with a hint of wry humor, "It was one of those *veiled* threats."

"Veiled?" said Lisa.

"You know," Arth continued, "He said it was a misunderstanding and all. I guess the Old Man decided to give him another chance."

∞

The solid centerline of the desolate state road warned us of the possibility of oncoming traffic in the other lane. But we hadn't seen traffic of any kind since the sun went down on this undeveloped stretch of land.

"Guess what I got," said Lisa.

"An FBI file?"

"How would I get an FBI file? No, I copied some pages out of Pete Dooley's notebook."

"That spiral notebook he's always carrying around? You snoop!"

"Well, after everything he's been saying, I think I'm justified."

"Okay, you're not a snoop," I said with giddy excitement. "You're a spy! What does it say?"

Lisa reached under her seat and I clicked on the interior light. She read from Dooley's longhand notes:

Ungodly advertisers. Stained with blood and ink. Lithograph wax polymer vs. soap made from animal fat and ashes, dripping down the sides of sacrificial altars, flows into the river where primitive women wash garments — the discovery of soap. A sign from God. Cleanliness next to Godliness. A command to remove the unclean marks of sin. Washed in blood. Eat the heart. Teflon is made from fluorocarbons (fluorine + carbon), carbon is the basis of all life, found in the burnt ashes of life, but Teflon is synthetic. Reagan called 'Teflon President' 'Synthetic President' shall rise, as wounded but lives, synthetic life — the beast! Repels water unnaturally! Sanctions Light Bending Technology for big business campaign contributions, top brass, polished brass, military brass, sanction sacrificial sign. Clean the world in the purity of a blazing Patmos vision.

120

"My God," I said.

"And the irony of it is, that's probably not how soap was discovered."

I just looked at her.

"Soap," she said. "Probably wasn't discovered by animal fat dripping down an altar."

I still couldn't think of anything to say.

"According to my chemistry professor," she added. "But, hey, he could be wrong."

∞

The next morning, as Lisa and I walked from the break room toward our respective cubicles, we noticed Arth leaving Mr. Thompson's office at the far end of the room. He walked to the nearby exit that led into a hallway, which formed a right angle to our oblong office, and gave us a quick, sideways tip of his head to indicate we should follow him.

In the hallway, we caught up with Arth as he entered an elevator.

"I'm on my way to the hotdog vendor on the corner," he said. "Care to join me?"

As the elevator doors closed, I said, "Arth, you know that old saying about trying the same thing over and over, expecting to get a different result?"

"It's a hell of a thing," he said.

"I've tried to pinpoint the moment Lisa and I decide to drive to Kingsland…" but my voice trailed off with the sudden realization I must be having blackouts.

"It's like being on a Mobius strip," said Arth.

"You, too?" I said.

"Sure, me too. For all I know, it could be the whole damn world by now."

"A what?" asked Lisa. "What did you just say?"

"A Mobius strip," explained Arth, "Is a strip of paper that only has one side. You make one by taking strip of paper, giving it a half-twist, and then taping the ends together. You can draw a straight line down the middle of it and cover what would ordinarily be both side of the paper, without ever lifting your pen off the paper."

"Your line meets itself and starts over again," I added.

"Maybe," said Arth only half-seriously, "Maybe you're hitting the bump where the ends are taped together, and that's where you forget and start over again."

"Why doesn't American Wage stop it?" I asked.

"American Wage isn't doing it," said Arth. "We stopped that shit almost as soon as we began."

"Pressure from the FBI?" asked Lisa.

"Hell, no. Man, if Granddad wants to do something, the FBI or the devil himself couldn't stop him. He got out of it for one simple reason. He says it's not ethical. And possibly dangerous."

"Then why did we have to be interrogated?"

"So I could get in there and find out what the FBI knows. They don't believe us, anyway. They think we're still experimenting on the sly, and from the way things are going, it's pretty obvious that some of the other insurance companies are still using the technology."

"Who?" asked Lisa. "And why did you let me go on thinking we were only stopping temporarily?

"Well, the FBI doesn't have to know everything. Granddad says we're playing our cards close to our chest."

"But why?" she asked.

"If the FBI were convinced that we weren't using the light-bending technology, their next step would be to ask us to work with them to find out who's screwing around with it."

"Well, why don't you?" asked Lisa, puzzlement ringing in her voice.

"It's complicated," said Arth, taking a pack of Camels from his pants pocket, pulling out a cigarette and perching it behind the top of his ear. "The technology is not illegal. Yet. Just because we don't use it doesn't mean we're gonna start a crusade and start snitching on fellow business people."

"Not illegal?" I said.

"Oh, some Congressman has introduced a bill to make it illegal, but now the politicians have to debate it, change it up a few times, and vote on it, so it might take a while."

"What is there to debate?" I asked. "Freakin' Ponce de Leon's campsite is next to the Riverfront Mall! Cavemen are working at the docks, for God's sake!"

"Yeah," said Arth. "And industries have been polluting rivers for years, but they have lobbyists who persuade the government not to stop them. Did you know that GM is building a functional electric car, and California is talking about passing a zero-emissions law?"

I had to ask, "Is it true that the oil companies buy up all the patents to electric cars?"

"I don't know about that," he said. "But I do know the oil companies have lobbyists, and I'm sure Global Interlinear has them, too."

"How can they…" Lisa started to ask, when the elevator doors opened into the lobby on the first floor.

Arth placed the cigarette in his mouth and said, "We're working on it. I'm working on it."

We walked through the lobby and Arth was lighting his Camel before we even got through the revolving door to the sidewalk.

Suddenly he said, "Oh, shit."

"What's the matter?" I asked.

"I left my wallet in my jacket pocket," he said, slapping at all his empty pockets and talking through smoke as he held the cigarette in his teeth. "Damn."

I reached for my wallet automatically, but only had two dollars.

"I got two bucks," I said.

"My purse is locked in my desk," said Lisa.

"Tell you what," said Arth to me. "You fly, I'll buy."

"You were gonna buy, anyway," I said.

"Yeah, but.." he held up his lit cigarette. "I can't go in with this."

"No problem, man," I said.

"My jacket is lying on the window sill in Mr. Thompson's office. The wallet's in the inside breast pocket. I'll go ahead and order for us."

"Two dogs," I said. "Slaw, onions, and mustard. And a Coke," and I was on my way back through the revolving door, striding across the lobby toward the elevator.

Moments after I stepped off the elevator on the 19th floor, a high-pitched wail practically punched me with its blunt loudness. Fire alarm.

A stream of people jostled against me, pouring out from the office as I tried to go back in.

Mr. Thompson met me with a jovial greeting, "You're going the wrong way! Fire drill!"

"I'm coming," I said. "Arth asked me to get his coat."

Mr. Thompson and I had to turn sideways, facing each other, as other employees crowded past us on either side.

"His coat?! Ain't he got five more?"

I laughed, too, edging past the big man into the room as he edged past me in the opposite direction.

"He left his wallet in the pocket," I said, looking back.

As Mr. Thompson followed the last of the evacuees into the hallway, I thought I heard him mumble, "Probably got five o'them, too."

I found Arth's coat in Mr. Thompson's office, on the long shelf in front of the plate glass window, between a potted cactus and a bowling trophy. I wondered what it would look like to see everybody leaving the building all at once, because of the fire drill.

I looked down at the sidewalk. The American Wage Building fills an entire city block. The sidewalk and street below me were empty and I realized that this was that back of the building. Everyone would be exiting from the front and side doors. Looking down to the far right, I could see the corner where the hotdog vendor always set up his cart.

But what I saw was horrifying.

The hotdog man lay motionless on the ground, his white "soda-fountain" diner's cap knocked crooked on his head. Lisa was struggling against two burly, overall-clad *Austras* as they carried her into the side door of an old, gray Volkswagen van. Arth was nowhere in sight. For all I knew, maybe he was already in the van.

I snatched up the telephone receiver and frantically dialed 911, but something was wrong. I heard no ring tone. I pressed the hang-up button for a second and listened again. No dial tone. The phone was dead.

The van lurched forward from the corner, moving from right to left, passing directly below me. Before it reached the end of the block, it turned abruptly toward our building and disappeared into the entrance of our parking garage. They were in this very building!

Running into the hallway, I found the elevator doors unresponsive. The *down* button didn't light up when I pushed it. The doors wouldn't open. This made no sense, as I clearly remembered the big deal they made during orientation, that American Wage had one of the new, state-of-the-art elevators, certified fireproof and operational in the event of a fire. Nevertheless, it was not working now.

The only thing left to do was take to the stairs, hurtling down two or three steps at a time.

A noise made me pause on the flight of steps between the third and fourth floor. Leaning on the bannister, breathing hard in my sweaty white shirt, I heard heavy footsteps approaching from below. I glanced cautiously over the railing and was startled to see two

Austras, a male and a female, lumbering up the steps. First I saw the tops of their heads, so close to me, spellbinding with those mythic, ape-like brows that turned slowly upward as they approached the turn. They wore overalls and the female had a rifle strapped over her shoulder. They turned the corner and scowled at me. I wondered if I should try speaking to them.

The female *Austra* unshoulderd her rifle. I bolted from the stairwell, into the hallway on the 3rd floor. The first room on the right was the Mail Room, the first place I had worked at American Wage Insurance Company. In that room, I saw one last chance to reach Lisa.

The whole building had a series of moving tracks inside the walls. You could put a plastic bin full of mail into an opening on one floor and set the code for another floor, and the bin would ride on the clanking mechanical rollers up or down the track to whatever floor you sent it. I went to the opening in the Mail Room and carefully climbed in.

I was careful not to get my foot or hand caught and crushed in the rollers on the moving track, but I forgot about the accursed symbol of corporate slavery, my necktie, and right away, my tie was seized by the machinery and my face was being pulled down toward the metal rollers. It was rumbling loudly and smelled of oil and I was choking and gripping at my shirt collar. I wanted to stay calm and untie the damn tie but my fingers wouldn't fit into the tightening knot. I was squatting with one foot on either side of the moving track, so I took a deep breath and stood up using all the strength in my legs. With a rip, the tie shredded loose. Standing up, I quickly slipped the remains of the tie off over my head and tossed it down into a plastic mail bin, which clattered between my feet and on down the line to I-don't-know-or-care-where.

Slowly, carefully, I made my way along the path with the machine noise rattling loudly through the corridors. I climbed down, floor after floor. They had some metal ladders for mechanics to use whenever the track needed fixing.

At last I came to a ledge which overlooked the basement where Pete Dooley, wearing a black hooded robe, had Lisa on the sacrificial alter, naked and helpless on the stone slab. She was conscious, eyes open, possibly in shock, or drugged, looking at the knife in the robed priest's hand. Four *Austras*, two on each side of the stone slab Lisa, held her arms and legs.

They chanted *Alpha, Omega*, backwards.

"Ahhhh, Flahhhhh, Ahhhhh, Gaamo!"

The end…the beginning…

The aroma of coffee and blood almost got to me. I thought for a second I wanted to join them. The one thing that clicked me out of my trance was that I wanted Lisa for myself.

I had no idea how to extricate Lisa from this bizarre predicament. Mindless, no-option determination kept me moving, hanging briefly from the ledge by my hands and then dropping several feet to the floor of the print shop, All eyes turned toward me. Rising to my feet, I tried to speak in a tone of reasoning and assurance, but found it difficult to catch my breath.

"Pete," I said. "Pete Dooley. What…uh…what's going on?"

If only I could get close enough to grab Lisa and pull her away from the immediate danger of the knife in Dooley's hand. The *Austras* listened intently to our conversation. The four of them turned their heads in unison to look at whoever was speaking. I noticed that they had relaxed their grip on Lisa, now barely touching her arms and legs.

"You ask me what's going on," said Dooley flatly. "You should know, being partly to blame. And so is she. And so is the greed of big business. And for that, a sacrifice must be made to cleanse time itself, to make time whole again."

"We all want to solve the problem," I said. "We can work together."

"We cannot work together. She saw to that."

"Well, but…please, if I can just talk to you for a minute…"

"A minute?" said the dark-hooded Dooley. "You might well ask for a *minute*. I am here to restore the order of minutes!"

He raised the knife over Lisa's chest.

"As Abraham offered Isaac for slaughter," said Dooley, "I offer this lamb!"

"Pete!" I shouted, running toward the alter, but I couldn't get there fast enough.

He plunged the knife downward, but the movement was abruptly halted by the firm grip of the caveman standing to his right. The *Austra's* large hand slowly pulled Dooley's arm upward, away from where the very tip of the blade had pierced Lisa's chest superficially.

Dooley looked with trembling awe at the prehistoric man and proclaimed, "As the Lord spared Abraham from taking the life of his son, so have I been spared by this noble giant who walked on earth, created in the very image of God!"

The *Australopithecus* jerked violently on Dooley's arm, hurling him backwards. Dooley screamed in pain and fell in a heap on the floor, entangled in his black robe. He didn't move.

I walked toward Lisa, not too fast, arms at my sides, head slightly bowed, trying to look non-threatening. The two *Austras* closest to me parted casually and allowed me to pass between them. I picked Lisa up with one arm under her back and the other arm under her knees. Pete Dooley's agenda was obviously not as important to his "assistants" as it was to him. I now recognized the sacrificial slab as an original 1901 limestone lithography stone, used by Leonetto Cappiello, the Italian poster artist.

Lisa looked into my eyes as I carried her toward the exit.

A noise made me look back. A female *Austra* held out a brown paper shopping bag with the Banana Republic logo on the side. Lisa's clothes were in the bag. I took the bag and started to say "Thank you," but who knew what noise or action on my part would set off a bad turn of events. I just took the bag and walked through the exit, into the parking garage.

My white 1980 Toyota Celica hatchback was a welcome sight, still waiting where I had parked it that morning. I placed Lisa on the hood of the car and reached into my pocket, relieved to feel the car keys.

"Where are my clothes?"

"Right here, in this bag. Come on, get in the car, quick."

I took her arm and practically pushed her into the passenger seat.

"Help me get dressed," she said, sitting sideways in the car with her feet still on the concrete floor of the garage.

I dropped the bag of clothes on her lap, lifted her legs, and rotated them into the car.

"Watch out," I said. "I'm shutting the door."

On the far side of the garage, three silhouettes appeared in the rectangle of light that was the street entrance to the parking garage. They ran toward us. Arth and the two FBI agents who called themselves Leonard and Skinnerd. Instead of biker jackets they wore suits. Leonard carried what appeared to be a tranquilizer gun and Skinnerd brandished an automatic pistol.

"Is Lisa okay?" asked Arth, peering through the windshield as she struggled to pull on her panties.

"Where were you earlier?" I asked.

"Walked around the corner to the newsstand."

"For real?"

"Why does no one believe I read the paper? Look, as you may have gathered, the shit's hitting the fan. I suggest you and Lisa drive up to Kingsland, Georgia. The submarine base is safe and they know what's going on. If we can't reverse this time fragmentation, I'll probably join you tomorrow."

The same bleak stretch of old Florida Highway A1A, running through a vast, undeveloped Florida swamp with nothing in sight for miles.

As we drove, we saw phantoms of gas stations and hotels and casinos. They appeared like mirages, but we knew they were from the future, things not yet built but trying to fade into the picture in the wavy time-lit night, like looking through heated air.

Lisa reached up and turned off the interior light because she had nothing more to read.

"I can't see out my window with that light glaring," she said.

The car sputtered to a stop. The bright red little engine light glowed on the darkened dashboard.

"Shit!" I said.

"Wait," said Lisa. "There was an opening back there!"

"An opening?"

"Through the bushes, a path or something."

"I've never noticed an opening."

We pushed the Toyota backwards to an almost hidden little dirt road leading off into some trees and sea oats. A middle path, neither forward nor backward, previously unseen because of the interior light glaring on the window.

I steered with one hand, walking beside the car, pushing against the doorframe with my other hand. Lisa pushed from the front. The car rolled backwards, off the pavement and onto the dirt path. It rolled downhill, bumping over small rocks and tree roots, until it came to a stop near a medium sized house with no lights on.

The house was deserted. It sat lower than the road and trees and brush, virtually hidden. Around back, the ground sloped gently upwards until it was buttressed by a concrete seawall. Looking down over the seawall was like standing on a small cliff beside the ocean, with waves lapping down below, and then nothing but ocean, as far as the eye could see. Lisa was so tired, I carried her into the house.

We have lived here forever now. The white 1980 Toyota Celica sits in the same spot forever. The trunk is open and full of soil with flowers growing in it. We will never get in that car again. We grow vegetables in the yard and eat oranges from a tree. Sometimes I fish.

We don't know how the rest of the world is doing. I don't know if we are aging. Lisa looks the same to me as always.

We heard on the radio that the American Wage Insurance Company, under the direction of Arthur Hampton, Sr. (Arth's grandfather), became the first insurance company to voluntarily discontinue the use of Light Bending, based on moral and ethical grounds. Not long after they severed their relationship with Global Interlinear, American Wage became insolvent due to excessive hurricane losses, and a larger company absorbed them. It seems unfair that that's what they got for taking the high road. Our young friend, Arth Hampton III, made the news a couple of weeks later when he won the first-place trophy in a prestigious yacht race.

A Crossroads in 1979-1980 U.S. military deal. In retrospect, Carter's blues, rising fuel prices, if continued, could have eliminated the same old stretch of terror road.

Then we stopped listening to the radio. We don't want to know what the corporations are doing, or who is President. We don't want to know anything. We just like living here forever.

End

The Darker Green Cemetery
A new story by Bill Ectric
August 21, 2024

It was 1965. Nobody had cell phones. We couldn't just call for help.

When I was eight years old, I saw a TV show about folklore and ghost stories of the Appalachian Mountains, close to where I lived. My friend Roger saw the same show, and he lived near a cemetery. We asked our parents if we could camp out in Roger's backyard. They said yes but be sure you do this and don't do that and blah, blah.

Not only were the front gates of the cemetery locked at night, but police cars also cruised the boulevard in front of the place at all hours, with those searchlights shining through the bars, looking for *goings on*. We knew of another entrance, but up to this point in our eight-year-old lives, we had been scared to try it.

Roger's backyard was enclosed by a split rail wooden fence. At the back of the property, we could climb over the fence, walk through a grove of trees, and down a steep rocky trail. The trail forked, and the path to the left went down and around, like a section of spiral staircase, but formed naturally in rock. As you turned the last corner at the bottom, you saw the gate to the Darker Green, too twisted to be seen from the boulevard. Some older kids told us about sneaking into the cemetery on a dare, and one kid was literally scared to death, but that turned out to be false. A janitor at school told a bunch of us that he could hear sighing and moaning when the thick fog rises from the ground in the graveyard. He said that the word "spirit" means "breath" and fog over a graveyard meant restless spirits were trying to ascend.

We set up my tent in Roger's backyard. Next, we filled up about thirty balloons with water from the garden hose, until each balloon swelled big enough to burst and soak somebody when it hit them. We stacked them in a wheelbarrow, bulging against each other like they wanted to pop on the spot. The wheelbarrow sat sideways in front of the tent door, with enough room for us to get in and out. We knew that if anyone wanted to raid us, they would come from behind, up the other fork in the path from the ballfield, carrying their water balloons in pillowcases or back packs.

"Let's fill a balloon with sour milk and pee."

"How would we even do that?"

"Like this," I said. "Look. Instead of turning off the water at the spicket, you crimp the hose while the water's running, like this, two or three feet from the open end. I was using a C clamp because my hand got so tired, but it wore a hole in my daddy's hose. Anyway, you bend the hose tight enough to stop the water flow. Pour off the excess water from the short end, like so. Now you can pour sour milk, pickle juice, bitters, one-of-a-kind tinctures, whatever. Stretch the balloon snug around the threads and hold it tight, like so, and unbend the hose. You'll get some water mixed in but that doesn't diminish the effectiveness of the missile."

"No, no, it's not good form."

"Good form?"

"Ed Clayburg got hit in the face by a dirty balloon, by a kid from Weymouth. Had to have his eyes irrigated or he could have gone blind."

"What was in it?"

"They never analyzed it. Weymouth has that quarry where human bones floated up, so…"

"Well, I let Toby hold some comics, on loan, and he gave them to his brother, who won't give them back, and I'm pissed at both of them. If I see him in the Darker Green I'll bean him good."

We called the cemetery the Darker Green. The proper name was Dakher Green Cemetery. In the 1850s, a guy named Dakher Green became a wealthy railroad baron. His railroads competed with the Vanderbilts. But for reasons unknown, he suddenly sold his business and retired a wealthy man. The rumor was that one of his trains killed a child. He dedicated a large parcel of land to become Dakher Green Memorial Park, but in time it became a cemetery. The dead needed the room.

Sundown.

Nightfall.

Roger and I sat in the tent with a lantern-style flashlight and two decks of cards, practicing card tricks on a table extension from the middle of his dining room table. Roger had a smaller flashlight hanging from his belt.

"If they don't raid us, we should raid them."

"Yeah, Toby's already said he's camping out with Russ on Penniman."

"When are we going down to the cemetery?"

"Let's play blackjack and wait for some action."

We were playing blackjack, drinking Cokes and eating peanuts, dropping the shells into a bucket, when the first two enemy water balloons thudded loudly and burst on the back of our tent.

"Crapola!"

We bolted out the tent door and grabbed water balloons from the wheelbarrow. Roger was winding up like a Big-League pitcher. I hesitated and looked. There was Toby himself, in front of the trees, partly hidden by the fence rails. Roger hurled his balloon like a rocket. I threw mine, aiming for Toby's face to keep from hitting the fence. Roger's balloon missed Toby and hit a tree, bursting on impact. Mine found its mark, splattering all over Toby's head and back as he ran away.

We ran back to the wheelbarrow. Hidden by the tent, we picked up two more water balloons, and peeked around the corner. I walked out into view, looking for a response. Looking for a movement of any kind.

"That's it?"

"No battle? He just ran?"

We got ambushed.

Two kids had brazenly entered Roger's front lawn from the street. They walked around to the backyard and pelted us from behind. It felt like slow-motion. I heard the slap of a balloon hitting Roger's back, bounce-wriggle-bounce, and as the water exploded on Roger's back, I saw the other balloon coming right at me. I tried to catch it, but splash! The thing burst on my arms, chest, and face. The two kids were laughing.

Roger ran toward them, with his balloon already in both hands, winding up, shouting "Trespass! Trespass!" which sounded wrong and made me laugh.

The two kids had what looked like a sheet with balloons piled on it, carrying it between them, holding corners together on each side. They started to run away, but it was too cumbersome. One kid dropped his side of the sheet and water balloons rolled all over the ground, some bursting.

Wound up for the pitch, Roger let fly and he beaned the smaller kid with his fast balloon.

He must have shouted 'trespass' too loud, because a light came on inside his house. A side door opened, and his dad stepped out onto a small porch. Now, both kids had dropped the sheet of balloons and were running toward Roger and me, away from the grownup instinctively.

Roger and I still hadn't been down to the Darker Green.

I surprised myself when I said, "Follow me.'"

I led Roger and the other two kids, climbing over the fence, and down the steep rocky path to the left.

There it was in front of us. An iron gate, framed by a stone archway, under a moonlit night.

I tried the gate, and it opened. The four of us entered the graveyard, and I closed the gate behind us.

"Man, I soaked you guys good," said Russ.

"Let's hide" said the other kid, which turned out to be Russ's little sister.

"Did you throw a balloon?" Roger asked her.

"She can't throw."

"I can, too! Let's hide, that man is coming."

"I don't think my dad will come all the way down here. He's probably back in bed."

"What was that noise? He *is* coming down here. You hear it?"

The vertical supports of the stone archway were each wide enough for two kids to hide behind.

"My name is Nancy. What's yours?"

"Whit."

Nancy and I were standing behind one side of the archway. A wispy fog was swirling slowly from the ground. We stared at it and looked at each other. A light hit me in the face from Roger's flashlight. Then he shined the light on Nancy.

"Turn it off," I hissed.

"Nobody's coming," said Roger. "Come on, let's walk through the Darker Green."

"Yeah," said Russ.

Roger and Russ walked out from behind the other pillar.

"The fog is getting more."

"Getting what?"

"More is floating up."

"It's okay, Nance."

Roger said, "Look at that" and shined his light on a life-size stone monument, chiseled into the form of an angel, with its wings folded down around its body and its head bowed. The four of us stood there, mesmerized by the artist's vision, until fog slowly made it disappear before our eyes.

"The fog is so thick."

"We should go back to your house, Roger. Hey man, I'm sorry about the water balloon."

Roger laughed and said, "I don't care, man. It's just water. But we got your other guy. We drenched Toby."

"Oh, man, we almost forgot about Toby! Where is he?"

"I thought he came down here," I said. "He must have taken the other path."

We were slowly strolling through the cemetery, Roger shining his flashlight on various monuments, mausoleums, and markers. We saw a marble engraving of a bearded man laying on a slab, one hand holding a lever of some kind. When the fog covered the hand and lever, we heard sounds like metal scraping against metal.

"That sounds like my hamster wheel," said Nancy.

But as the sound got closer, it got deeper and more rhythmic.

Roger unclipped his flashlight and turned it on. The fog rolled like smoke in the flashlight beam. Beads of moisture reflected a wall of light back at us like high beams in the fog.

"Did you guys feel it?"

"What?"

"Like the ground moving?"

I did feel vibrations in my feet.

"Stop," said Russ. "Nance. We're standing right here for a minute."

"Why?" she asked.

"Can *you* see? Because *I* can't see."

Crying.

"It's okay sis, just keep holding my hand."

I think she said, "I'm not scared" but I could barely hear her over the wind and mechanical rumbling.

I walked ahead of the others and almost tripped on a railroad track. Years ago, this place was a train station before it was a cemetery. I stepped up onto one of the rails and balanced on it, holding my arms out like a tightrope walker. After a few steps I slipped on something wet and fell hard on my back. My breath was knocked out.

"Is that Whit laying down over there?"

"What?"

I held up one arm and moved it weakly. Roger's flashlight beam hovered on me for a moment and then moved further up the track.

The wind and thunder seemed further away now.

"Oh my God," he said, running past me. He said it again, "OH my God…Russ! You and Nance stay back."

"What's the matter?"

I was sitting up, trying to stand up, but trying to catch my breath.

"Russ listen," said Roger. "Take your sister and go to my house. Knock on the door, ring the bell, but tell my dad that Toby is hurt really bad."

I stood up and looked where Roger was shining his light. Toby was laying halfway across the tracks.

His head and chest were on one side of a rail. His stomach and legs were on the other side of the rail. Blood glistened all around him. My knees felt week and I felt sick. He was cut in half on the train track.

I woke up with a jolt from the ammonia inhalant that Roger's dad was holding under my nose.

I started crying.

"It's okay, man. He's right over there."

"Yeah, dude, I'm right over here."

"Alive?"

When the gravel under a railroad track starts to wear out, they replace it with new gravel. Sometimes they use a heavy-duty machine called a ballast undercutter to dig the old gravel out from under the rail. That process had been started here, but for whatever reason, it was never finished before the station was retired from service. Toby was a lank fellow, able to fit under the rail where enough gravel was missing, making him appear cut in two. He had some gruesome slick red balloon tincture of his own.

"Hey, can somebody help me out?"

Toby was stuck under the rail. Russ reached down and offered his hands. Roger was shining his flashlight on them.

"Pull," said Toby. "Hard as you can… Ow! No, it's okay. Pull…Ow!"

Roger said, "Try pulling him out by his ankles. Toby, you got anything in your pockets, or clipped to your belt? Something is probably getting caught."

Even further up the track, I saw a black hole. It was a real tunnel entrance, carved into the side of the mountain. We heard a stark whistle, the pounding of pistons, and the tunnel was belching smoke. A Ghost Train killed Toby.

No, I'm just kidding. There was no train, ghost or otherwise.

"Wait, it feels like my pants are coming off," said Toby.

"You boys figure it out. I'm going up to the house." Roger's dad.

Ghost train.

Also by Bill Ectric

Tamper Illustrated

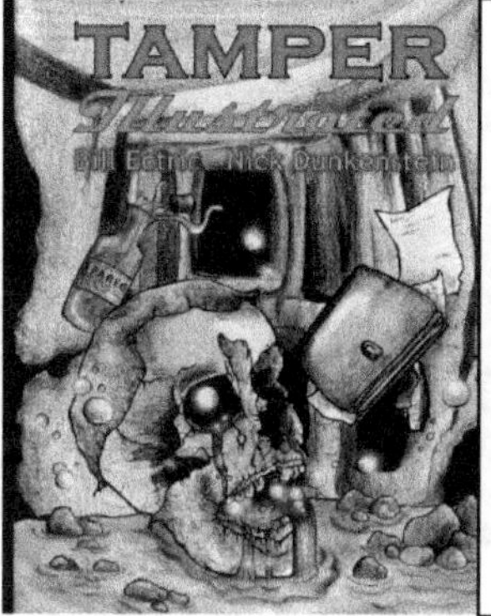

Growing up in the 1960s with strange noises in the basement, dark magic in the leaves, young love, the Shaver Mystery, psychedelic drugs, and alien brain signals that *tamper* with your brain.

Steve Aylett: A Critical Anthology

"I particularly liked Bill Ectric's lovely description of exploring Aylett's treasures. He is one of those modest people who has so much under the surface, yet doesn't let on about his erudition. This book is, I think, primarily his brainchild, but he and Wilson must have complemented each other to produce such a fine, and subversive outcome." - Anna Tambour

Anna Tambours writes satire, fables, and other literary fiction and poetry. Her novel *Crandolin* was shortlisted for the 2013 World Fantasy Award. Her "The Jeweller of Second-hand Roe" -won the 2008 Aurealis Award for best horror short story. Tambour is also a photographer and writes about photography. She lives in Australia.

Thank you for reading Time Adjusters and Other Stories.

billectric